BLUE HELL

GREG F. GIFUNE   SANDY DeLUCA

JOURNALSTONE
YOUR LINK TO ARTIST TALENT

ISBN: 978-1-950305-67-4 (sc)
ISBN: 978-1-950305-68-1 (ebook)
Library of Congress Catalog Number: 2020952582

First printing edition: March 5, 2021
Published by JournalStone Publishing in the United States of America.
Cover Design and Layout: Don Noble
Edited by Sean Leonard
Proofreading and Interior Layout by Scarlett R. Algee

JournalStone Publishing
3205 Sassafras Trail
Carbondale, Illinois 62901

JournalStone books may be ordered through booksellers or by contacting:
JournalStone | www.journalstone.com

As always, to all my friends, fans, and readers all over the world, for your continued enthusiasm and support, my deepest thanks. And thanks to my longtime dear friend and colleague, Sandy DeLuca, without whom this work would have been impossible to pull together into anything remotely worth doing.

—Greg F. Gifune

Special thanks to Greg F. Gifune for believing in my writing—from the very beginning—and for the invitation to work with him on what eventually became BLUE HELL. And much love and appreciation to all those who have read my fiction through the years, and continue to do so.

—Sandy DeLuca

For Jon K. Kupchik (aka Jon Recluse)
December 7, 1963 – July 28, 2020
Rest well, my friend. See you on the other side.

BLUE HELL

PART ONE

MAPS OF CHANGE

"No one can tell what goes on in between the person you were and the person you become. No one can chart that blue and lonely section of hell. There are no maps of change. You just come out the other side. Or you don't."

—Stephen King, *The Stand*

CHAPTER 1

YOUR SOUL IS NO LONGER YOUR OWN.

He hears the voice, but it's the flames he remembers. Crawling up from the darkness, they appear suddenly and as if by magic, engulfing and devouring him before he realizes what's happening. The screams and pain rise in a frenzy of terror that explodes from some instinctual but hidden and forgotten chamber deep within him, then just as quickly, they're gone, replaced by a maddening and empty silence.

And finally, his hunger is sated.

Despite the window in his hospital room, this is a place of shadows. As it gradually comes into focus, he studies the still and overcast day just beyond the pane of glass, and the nearly empty parking lot and bleak gray cityscape beyond.

As if summoned directly from his nightmares, a light snow begins to fall.

"Do you remember the accident?"

This time the voice startles him. A different voice, a female voice, he follows it to a stern middle-aged woman sitting in a chair in the corner. Her back is razor-straight, her knees are together, and her gray hair is pulled up into a tight bun atop her head. She wears a pair of black eyeglasses, an ankle-length skirt, an old-fashioned blouse with a high neck and lacy sleeves, and sensible lace-up shoes. Along with her clipboard and fountain pen, it all conspires to give her the appearance of an early nineteenth century schoolmarm that has traveled through time to question him.

He waits, not yet certain if she's real or merely a remnant of the dark.

The woman looks up from her notes, or whatever it is she's scribbling on her clipboard pad. "Mr. Stringer?"

He clenches shut his eyes. When he opens them, she's still there.

"Do you remember the accident?" she asks again.

Flashes—hideous and obscene—dart across his mind's eye.

"Fire," Stringer says. His voice is weak and raspy and sounds like someone else. "The whole world was in flames."

"No." The woman's eyes narrow behind the thick lenses of her glasses. "There was no fire, Mr. Stringer. You were struck by a car. Do you remember?"

He thinks a moment. "I remember the flames but still being so…*cold*."

"As I say, there was no fire, Mr. Stringer, but the latter makes perfect sense. It was brutally cold that night, the worst in recent history. Per the police report, you ran into the street and directly into the path of an oncoming car. The driver stated you appeared to be quite disoriented and behaved as if you were running from someone."

Horrible growl-like whispers flood his mind, but they sound very far away and he can't decipher what they're saying. For that, he is grateful.

"Or perhaps some*thing*," she adds.

"How long have I been here?"

"Not too long. You only came awake late last night. You're extremely fortunate, Mr. Stringer. Although your injuries are relatively minor, you easily could've been killed. You've suffered some scrapes and bruises, along with a concussion, of course, but even that, according to the doctors, could've been far worse."

Stringer nods, though he has no idea what she's talking about.

"To be clear," the woman says, "you're suggesting you've no memory of the accident at this time?"

His body is sore, his head hazy. Still crawling his way out of a bad dream, he tries to remember but can't. Only the fire remains, the flames…the horrible screams and the bitter cold…

"Yes," he answers.

She watches him a moment, as if weighing the validity of his response. Eventually, her eyes lower to the clipboard and she jots something down. "And you know your name is Joseph Stringer, correct?"

"Yes, but…how do *you* know my name?"

"That is your name, isn't it?" she asks, perplexed. "Why wouldn't I be aware of it at this juncture?"

A voice—his voice—as if screamed from the far end of a long tunnel, distorts and echoes as it twists through his head.

Am I dead?

The woman watches him, awaiting his response.

"I'm sorry if I don't understand everything right away," he says, realizing he has no memory of her prior to noticing her in the chair. "Everything's still foggy."

"I'm sure it is." Her tone remains bureaucratic, void of warmth or emotion. "You were without identification at the time of the accident, and from your clothes and general appearance it was rather obvious you'd been having a difficult time beforehand."

He doesn't know what to say to this, so he remains quiet.

"I understand this can be a delicate issue, Mr. Stringer, but it is one we both need to be aware of right now. You do realize you're homeless, do you not?"

"Yes," he says grimly, though he can't remember much beyond that.

"I can assist you." She takes more notes. "I can help you transition."

"Transition?" he asks. "I don't understand."

"You will come to understand."

"I'm here to help you," she explains evenly.

He nods, although he's unsure of what to make of her.

"Of course, you're under no obligation, as it were, to accept my assistance," she tells him. "But it is unquestionably the wisest choice, Mr. Stringer. Living on the streets like some sort of wild animal is not the way to continue forward. I can arrange a place for you to live for the time being, but I'll need your decision immediately. I cannot force myself or my help upon you. I'm sure you understand."

He understands nothing. The cold returns, rattling him. Or perhaps it never left, for it is the fire he remembers, but the *cold* he feels right down into his bones.

He looks out the window again, watches the falling snow. It seems to be just a flurry, yet the ground is covered, and for the first time he notices a great amount of snow has been plowed into lines of enormous filthy piles on the far end of the lot. He's not sure why, but this frightens him.

"Mr. Stringer, are you willing to listen to me?" she asks.

"I am," he says softly.

"Would you like my assistance, then?"

Flashes of shadowy figures standing over him drift through his mind, cruel spirits lingering at the very edge of his perception.

"Yes, ma'am," he says softly. "I would."

CHAPTER 2

THE DEAFENING VIOLENT SCREECH OF A braking car tears through his head. The sound snaps him out of his trance, or whatever it was, and although he has no idea where he is or how he came to be here, as the sound fades and the darkness recedes, he also realizes he is not alone.

"Mr. Stringer?" The same woman from the hospital hovers nearby. She has added a long wool coat to her wardrobe, along with a plastic rain bonnet covering her hair and tied in place beneath her chin. "Are you still with me?" she asks, studying him with the predatory superiority of a hawk sizing up a field mouse.

He looks around, finds himself in a small apartment. "Yes, ma'am."

"You may call me Mrs. Milken."

A nearby bed is made up with inexpensive white sheets, a wafer-thin tan blanket, and a stained pillow, sans case. It looks terribly uncomfortable and impersonal, like it's been removed from an institution and left there mistakenly.

"Obviously the accommodations are basic and rather sparse," she says. "And it's not the best neighborhood. But it's preferable to the street or a shelter."

"Yes," Stringer says, taking in the equally uncomfortable looking chair in the corner, and an old, chipped cast-iron radiator that takes up nearly the entire adjacent wall. "I'm grateful. It'll be fine."

Mrs. Milken purses her lips and gives a curt nod.

Stringer suspects this is the closest the woman ever comes to smiling.

The floor is bare wood, scuffed and scarred, and the empty walls are a dull, faded white. The ceiling is the same and outfitted with a basic overhead bowl-style light fixture, the bottom quarter of which is filled with the carcasses of numerous insects long dead.

A nearby alcove houses a modest kitchen with a small metal table and two chairs, an apartment-sized stove and refrigerator, and a sink, above which two pressboard cupboards hang. Opposite that are the only windows, two of them side-by-side and adorned with dusty and discolored Venetian blinds.

Night has fallen over the city, and beyond the dirty panes of glass, a steady ticking against the windows reveals the earlier snow has turned to rain.

"Is there a bathroom?" Stringer asks.

Somewhere down on the street, three stories below, a car alarm blares.

"One per floor, with a toilet, sink, and shower, located at the end of the hall." She stares at him as if she expects a response, or perhaps resistance, her eyes magnified by her thick eyeglass lenses. When neither arrives, she continues. "The entire building—all three floors—consists of identical units. Most are occupied at this time but…people…come and go here."

"I understand," he says, even though he's not sure he does.

Sudden strobe-like flashes come to him, striking like an assault. A face partially concealed in darkness and wrapped in plumes of breath hitting cold night air leers at him.

Is he dead?

Stringer grimaces, afraid the fear will overtake him, but it all drifts away. Like smoke, he thinks, spiraling away to nothing.

"You look as if you're having a headache, and frankly, some confusion as well," Mrs. Milken says. "Are you certain you're all right, Mr. Stringer?"

He runs a hand over his face. "I'm still a little out of it, that's all."

"You did suffer a concussion, remember. If you're experiencing any further symptoms, please let me know and we'll go back to the hospital for more tests. One can never be too careful when it comes to head injuries." She moves closer. "The mind, while complex, can be extremely...*delicate*."

You have no idea, he thinks. *Or do you know even more than I?*

"For now I suggest you just settle in," she says. "The rest will come."

"Will I see you again?"

A subtle but unmistakable smirk curls her lips. "We'll see."

Stringer can't be sure if her response is threatening or if his jumbled mind has simply interpreted it that way. "Is it all right if I ask you something else, Mrs. Milken?"

"Of course," she says.

The car alarm finally ceases. Sounds of the city fill the brief silence.

"Why are you doing this for me?"

Mrs. Milken walks to the door. With her back to him, she says, "Only a select few ever come here. You are among them."

"But I mean, why me?"

Slowly, she looks back over her shoulder at him. Mrs. Milken's eyes have become much darker. Black instead of brown now, they no longer appear wholly human. Deep in his gut Stringer feels the fear slither closer and coil around him, tightening, smothering, and slowly squeezing the life from him. He takes a step back and looks away, his face twisted in horror.

"It's my job," she says. "It's what I do."

Despite his fear, he follows the sound of her voice and forces himself to look at her again.

Mrs. Milken's eyes have returned to normal.

"And trust me, Mr. Stringer, like the other lost souls here, you've *earned* your place."

CHAPTER 3

IS HE DEAD?

Owen didn't bother to look back at him. "Not yet."

Stringer shivered, watched their clouds of breath churn about like living veils before rising toward the open hold and escaping into the night air. If only he could fly too, just rise and slip away, glide through the sky with the effortless grace of a thrown stone skipping across the surface of the ocean.

Free…safe…

In the dark, and in this extreme cold, it was impossible to tell where their spirals of breath ended and the slowly falling garlands of snow began. With his cheap blanket pulled up under his chin, Stringer did his best to ward off another incoming wave of terror. His teeth chattered violently and he clenched his jaw, ignoring the pain in his feet and hands. "If we stay here, we'll die."

Owen finally looked back at him. "Don't you think I know that?"

He looked so big there in the darkness of the hold, arms wrapped around Tinker, holding the poor bastard close in an attempt to share whatever body heat he had left. His eyes blinked, lashes and brows crusted with ice and snow, his skin, even partially concealed in several days' growth of beard, so pale it looked as if all the blood had long since drained away. His lips had turned an odd shade of purple over the last few hours, *and Stringer knew he looked the same. Dying, slowly freezing to death in this frozen hell of ice and snow.*

"He's dead," Stringer said softly. "Tinker's gone, man."

* * * *

He comes awake from the nightmare like a drowning man flailing for the surface of the ocean. Sucking in an urgent rush of breath, he violently snaps upright, swinging punches at the darkness until he realizes where he is.

Rolling to the edge of the bed, Stringer plants his bare feet on the cold wood floor and takes a frantic look around, trying desperately to remember as much as he can. He thrusts his hands into a beam of moonlight breaking through the windows and segmented by the blinds. There's no blood.

Chest heaving, he sits shivering in the cold and wondering if that old radiator ever comes on. Unable to find a thermostat anywhere in the apartment, he assumes it must be controlled from a central location somewhere in the building, but he hasn't left his apartment yet so it's impossible to know for sure.

Stringer wonders what time it is. He doesn't wear a watch, and the only clock in the apartment is a small one on the stove, but it's broken. He knows it must be very late, though, as the city has quieted.

Much as the city ever does.

Wearing only his boxers and a sweatshirt, Stringer pulls the blanket free and wraps it around him as he stands and shuffles over to the windows. Dull city lights twinkle through curtains of snow blowing about, and three stories below, in an alley between a hardware store and an insurance agency, a fire burns in a metal barrel, sending occasional sprays of sparks high into the air. Three dark figures huddle around it. Stringer can't make out anything more than their silhouettes. He moves closer to the window and looks to the right. In the distance, the ocean rages, dark and menacing as the night that surrounds him. Fear surges from the pit of his stomach into the base of his throat like acid. Trembling, he turns his back to the windows. Attempting to dismiss his fear, Stringer tells himself the frigid temperature in the apartment is to blame.

In the dream, the dead man's name was Tinker, and there is something terribly familiar about that. The dream itself is familiar, but Stringer cannot yet make any sense of it or figure out why it frightens him so.

Standing in the dark and quiet apartment, he tries to remember the accident that led to his concussion and other injuries. Mrs. Milken insisted he was hit by a car, yet he has no memory of this. He closes his eyes and tries again, but all he sees are flames shooting up from the dark and engulfing him, burning him as he screams and cries for mercy.

Mercy, he thinks.

Something comes to him, some strand of memory, a vague scrap with no context, spoken in an eerie monotone.

Do not be merciful, but be just...

It's as if very long ago, in some distant and blurry past, he's heard these words before. They strike him as unfinished somehow.

Do not be merciful, but be just...

There's more, he's sure of it, he just can't remember the rest. If only he could recall where he heard it, or when, he might be able to put things together. With the answers continuing to elude him, Stringer sits on the edge of his bed, and shivering from the incessant cold, struggles to sort his thoughts.

"What's happening to me?" he whispers.

The night ignores his question.

But later, when he finally returns to sleep, his nightmares do not.

CHAPTER 4

OWEN HELD HIS FRIEND CLOSER, THE *body limp and the thin plumes of mist once seeping from his nostrils and open mouth no longer visible.*

"Tink?" He shook the man gently. "Tink, you hear me?"

"He doesn't hear anything anymore."

Owen laid the man back and carefully rested his head on the blanket of snow lining the bottom of the ship. "Tink?"

Stringer turned away, drew his knees in close to his chin, and wrapped his arms around his legs. Hugging himself tight, he battled another round of shivers.

"I'm sorry, Tink," Owen said in a loud whisper. "We should've gone south. I know that now. I should've listened to you, man, I should've. I thought we'd be all right. I didn't think it could be this bad. We should've gone south like we did last time, but I thought by morning we'd be all right. I had no way of knowing it would be so bad, you understand? Tink, you understand? Tink?"

"Take it easy, Owen." Stringer wiggled his toes inside what was left of his shoes. He could barely feel them. "And don't leave his eyes open, it's not right."

The big man reached down and shut Tinker's eyes.

Tinker had been smaller, thinner, weaker than the other two, and the elements had taken him apart faster. Out here, a person had to be strong, and in the short time Stringer had known Tinker, he was never physically fit. He'd been out too long, suffered too much, run into too many illnesses and problems men and women like them dealt with day in and day out. But this—this goddamn arctic winter—was too much. The best of the best would have trouble surviving it.

Tinker never stood a chance.

Neither does his other new friend Owen. Only he doesn't realize it yet.

* * * *

A steady knocking gradually drags Stringer from sleep. He rises slowly toward the light of consciousness, gliding up through muddy darkness until he breaks the surface and comes awake gasping for air. It feels as if he hasn't been breathing for some time, and has only now remembered how to do so.

As Stringer sits up and rubs his eyes, he realizes someone is knocking on the door. He looks to the windows. It is light out, but he can tell it's still early morning. "Hold on," he calls out groggily.

He remembers dreaming about Owen and Tinker, and while it still doesn't make much sense, it feels like maybe it's starting to come back to him.

The knocking becomes a pounding.

Shaking off the fear, Stringer rises to his feet, and ignoring the cold floor, moves to the door.

It is outfitted with a deadbolt and a chain lock, both of which are engaged. There is no peephole, so he leans against the door. "Who is it?"

When no answer comes, he asks again. With still no response, Stringer unlocks the deadbolt but leaves the chain on, then opens the door wide enough to peek out.

No one there, but a wrinkled brown paper bag sits on his doorstep.

Stringer pulls the chain free and steps out into the hallway. Empty and quiet, there aren't even any sounds of footfalls echoing from the staircase. There is one door directly across from him, which he assumes is to another apartment, and one at the end of the hallway, which is likely the bathroom. Neither has received a delivery.

He moves to the head of the stairwell and looks down. A spiral staircase winds dizzily to a small lobby three floors below. He thinks he sees a shadow, perhaps a silhouette moving quickly on the ground floor, but it sweeps by so quickly he can't be sure. With a sigh, Stringer returns to his apartment door, picks up the bag, and rummages through it.

He finds a bottle of spring water, a quart of milk, a loaf of hearty white bread, a plain ceramic mug, and a small tin of coffee. With another quick look around, he slips back inside, closing and locking the door behind him.

In the kitchen, he places the bag on the table and unpacks the items, lining them up in a neat row. *Strange*, he thinks. A hot cup of coffee does sound nice, but there's no sign of a coffeemaker. He checks the cupboards above the stove and finds one, along with a package of unopened paper filters. Otherwise, the cupboards are empty. A small and basic model, the coffeemaker appears to be new and unused. *About the only thing in this place that is*, he thinks.

After a quick setup, Stringer turns the coffeemaker on. As it comes to life, gurgling and trickling coffee into the carafe, he leaves the apartment and tries the door at the end of the hallway.

The tiled walls within are cracked, badly worn and thick with mold, but it is, in fact, a bathroom. The shower, a small boxy unit with a cheap plastic curtain, looks as if it hasn't been used in some time, and along with the sink and toilet is in desperate need of a thorough cleaning. A strong odor of urine fills the air, which reminds him why he came here in the first place.

While Stringer pees, he glances around the small room as a means of distraction. As he finishes up and flushes, he notices a single tile missing down near the baseboard next to the sink. Certain he can make out something written on that small square of wall, he crouches down for a closer look.

Crudely scratched into the drywall are two words.

HELP ME

CHAPTER 5

"WE CAN'T STAY IN THE SHIP," Stringer said, interrupting the cries of the wind.

"Ain't nothing but ice and snow out there." Owen fell back and settled against the side of the hold. "Where the hell we gonna go?"

"We stay here, we won't live the night."

Owen's dying eyes stared at him through the darkness and mist. "What makes you think we're gonna live the night anyway?"

"If we stay here we got no chance, Owen. None."

"Got none out there either, that's what I'm telling you."

"If we can make it far enough there's a chance."

"There ain't no—"

"A chance, goddamn it, that's all I'm saying. We'll have a chance." Stringer struggled back to his feet, his legs shaking so violently he wasn't sure they'd hold him. He reached out and steadied himself against the side of the hold, but his tattered gloves slid along the icy interior of the ship and he nearly fell. "In this temperature, with no food and no way to stay warm but for huddling together under these cheap-ass motherfucking blankets, we're done."

"But—"

"We stay another night, we die for sure."

Owen's stomach grumbled beneath the worn coat he'd wrapped himself in. "Whatever we do, we do together."

Stringer nodded. "We can make it, man. I know I just met you guys a few days ago, but believe me when I tell you I've been through this kind of shit before."

"Me too, but God Almighty, not nothing this bad."

"I know one thing for sure, this ship ain't going nowhere."

Both men chuckled.

"Been sitting too long," Stringer said, sighing. "Can't feel my legs and arms that good. We got to find better shelter, fucking heat. We got to try."

"You forget where the hell you're at? Where we supposed to find all that, you crazy bastard? You think I would've let us sit here in the bottom of this ship, you think I would've let Tink die down here if there was any chance out there in that storm?" A cloud passed over the moon, and the cramped space of the ship's hold grew a bit darker, washing Owen's face in shadow. "We should've gone south, man. Why the fuck didn't we just go south when we had the goddamn chance?"

"It's too late for all that now."

Owen glanced at his dead friend. "I could've just killed him with my bare hands, would've been faster, more merciful."

"It ain't your fault."

"Yeah," Owen said, as if remembering better days. "It is."

"Tink wasn't cut out for this shit."

"Ain't no human being cut out for this." Owen extended a hand. "No one should die like this. Not a goddamn bit of dignity in it."

Stringer took Owen's hand, felt still-powerful fingers curl around his own as he helped him to his feet. "You go on up and take a look around. I'm gonna...you know."

"Fuck, man, can't you just leave him alone?"

"He don't need that coat or vest no more, Owen. We do."

Owen nodded sullenly then turned away. "Hurry up."

* * * *

The world shifts, blurs, and tilts before slowly righting itself. As Stringer's vision comes into focus, the nightmare strands him on the bathroom floor, his back against the toilet, legs bent and trapped beneath him. Did he pass out?

Movement from the corner of his eye catches Stringer's attention. Still disoriented, he looks to the doorway to find a shockingly thin old man lurching past. Nude, and with a horseshoe of unruly white hair circling his otherwise bald, liver-spotted head, the man grimaces in torment, staggering away along the hallway like some horrifying creature, his gangly body contorted and twisted.

Stringer frantically frees his legs and gets back to his feet, just as the old man stumbles into the apartment across from his, the door slamming behind him.

His heart racing, Stringer hurries after him to the door, but stops short of attempting to open it. "Hello!" he calls out instead. "Who are you?"

Silence has returned to the building, but the old man has left behind a hideous stench. Stringer recognizes it immediately, because he's smelled it before. He can't remember when or where or even how he knows this, but he has no doubt what it is.

The stench of rotting human flesh is unmistakable.

Stringer slowly retreats until he feels the door to his apartment against his back. Reaching behind him, he turns the knob then slips inside but leaves the door open a crack. With memories of the horrifically gnarled old man flooding his mind, Stringer peers out across the hall.

Nothing further happens, so he closes the door and locks it.

His apartment smells of freshly brewed coffee, which is a welcome change from the stink in the hallway, but Stringer can't settle his nerves.

What the hell is this place? What's going on? Why is he having horrible nightmares that assault him even when he's awake, and why are they causing him to lose consciousness? And who is that tortured soul across the hall?

Stringer has no answers, so he returns to bed, assuring himself he'll just lay down a moment, clear his head and collect himself. But as he closes his eyes, he cannot prevent himself from being absorbed back into the darkness.

Black waves crash all around him, as if he's lost at sea in the dead of night. Though he tries, he cannot prevent himself from being pulled under.

The last thing he remembers is the waves taking him down.

CHAPTER 6

STRINGER WATCHED OWEN CLIMB THE LADDER *and disappear out onto the deck above. Icy flakes of snow pricked his eyes. He blinked them away and turned his attention to Tinker's body. As he crouched down, his knees ached and the same shooting pains he'd endured for hours fired up his spine and into his pelvis.*

"Nothing personal, bud," he said quietly. "If it was me lying there, I'd expect you to do the same."

Once he'd removed the old coat and torn vest from Tinker's body, he gave another quick look up and saw that Owen had wandered off along the deck and out of sight.

From the pocket of his jacket, Stringer removed a knife.

After cutting free a piece of Tinker's trousers, he poked at the dead man's thigh with the tip of the knife. It jiggled but remained intact. Human casing was stronger than it initially appeared. This time, using more force and leaning his weight into it, Stringer thrust the blade forward until it punctured the skin with a muffled snapping sound. Slowly pulling the blade free, he dipped it deeply into the soft flesh of Tinker's inner thigh.

He was starving. He'd been ravenous for days.

The blood, *he thought*, it might still be warm.

"Yes," he whispered.

Stringer lapped at the steel until he'd licked it clean. It tasted coppery, but he was so hungry. With famished abandon, he returned the blade to the wound, drew it across then down in a single savage slash, and lopped off a small chunk of meat from Tinker's thigh.

It fell into the palm of his free hand, and without looking at it Stringer pushed it between his lips, suckling the juices before taking it completely into his mouth. Something tingled behind his eyes, like the beginnings of a yawn, but he ignored it, bit down, chewed...and swallowed.

"It ain't no better than before!" Owen called from above. "Can't see shit!"

Stringer quickly returned the knife to his pocket, wiped his mouth, then slipped the vest on over his jacket. With the flavor of Tinker's blood still clinging to the roof of his mouth, still soaked into his tongue, still burning the base of his throat, he flung the coat over his shoulder and forced himself up the ladder.

* * * *

In a panic, Stringer bolts upright and launches himself from bed. Spitting on the floor, he pushes his hands into his mouth, runs them over his tongue and spits a second time. He finds no blood, no flesh.

Stumbling for the sink, he just makes it, vomiting once and then again.

Draped over the counter, Stringer spits out the last of the bile and tries to catch his breath. The smell of freshly brewed coffee fills the apartment. He'd forgotten about the coffee, but is now grateful for it, as the aroma distracts him from his nightmares and the awful taste in his mouth.

He pushes away from the sink and wipes his mouth with the back of his hand. As soon as the terrible dreams recede, the memories of the bathroom, the hallway, and the freakish old man take their place. There seems to be no respite from the horror here. Or is *he* the horror somehow, like a magnet drawing these things to him?

Stringer grabs the carafe and fills the mug with coffee. Upon returning the carafe to the burner, he shuffles over to the window. It's still light out, but no longer early morning. How long has he slept? he wonders. The snow is still falling, and it is accumulating now, blanketing the streets and buildings in white. There are few people below, most hurrying through the snow and cold, and when he looks to the ocean it is choppy, the waves furiously crashing about.

Something about those angry waves mesmerizes him.

He sips his coffee. It tastes good, and warms him. Stringer positions himself in the window so his angle allows him to watch the ocean awhile.

The longer he stares at those waves, the closer the answers to his hauntings creep. Yet maddeningly, they continue to dance along the periphery of his awareness, still just slightly out of reach.

Those waves and…the…the *cold*…the cold, vast ocean…

"Do not be merciful, but be just…"

Stringer whirls around and raises his hands, fully expecting someone to be standing behind him. The coffee spills, burns his wrist. "Goddamn it!"

He is alone in the apartment.

But that's not possible. This time the words were not in his mind. He *heard* them. A man's voice, clear as day and only a foot or two from his ear, it was spoken in monotone, eerily and as if by rote, but unmistakably real.

He's heard that voice before. In the hospital, he remembers.

Your soul is no longer your own.

Fearful he may spill the rest of the coffee, or worse, drop the mug and shatter it, Stringer places it on the counter and slowly backs away. "The fuck is happening," he mutters, bringing his hands to his head.

The apartment suddenly feels like a tomb closing in around him, pushing him deeper into his grave, down into the cold dirt. He needs to get out of here for a while, to clear his head and breathe some fresh air, maybe take a long walk in the snow and get a feel for the neighborhood. Stringer dresses, takes another quick swallow of coffee, then grabs his old coat and heads for the door.

Memories of that old man lurching about stop him in his tracks. Unlocking the door, he opens it just a crack and peers out into the hallway, craning his neck in one direction and then the other until he can see both ends of the hall and is satisfied no one is out there.

Once in the hallway, Stringer closes the door then hurries to the spiral staircase, holding the cold wooden bannister as he makes his way down two stories to the ground floor.

The sound of his footfalls echo through the open space, but otherwise the building remains deathly quiet. There are no windows here and limited light, so the staircase is dim and musty, the stairs scarred and the banister dirty. With no one else in sight, it's as if he's alone here. But he knows that isn't the case.

As Stringer reaches the lobby, he steps down into a small foyer, the floor a series of old and badly worn black and white tiles arranged to resemble a checkerboard. He knows he's been here before—how else would he and Mrs. Milken have gotten into the building—but he has no memory of it.

Before him are two large doors, the center panel glass and etched with what appears to be a series of butterflies. They seem oddly ornate in such an otherwise drab building, though like everything else here, they're in need of a thorough cleaning and look quite dated.

Beyond the doors, through the glass, Stringer watches the snow fall a moment. With a deep breath, he reaches for the handles and gives them a gentle push.

They rattle but do not give, so he tries pulling instead. Same result.

He tries again, shaking the handle harder this time, but it refuses to give.

"Sucks, right?"

Startled, Stringer looks behind him to find a young woman sitting on the bottom step of the stairs from which he's just come. With short black hair styled into a purposely mussed pixie cut, heavy black eye makeup, ruby lipstick and an entirely black outfit—blouse, jeans, Doc Martens boots—she gives him a wry smile and stabs an unlit cigarette into the corner of her mouth.

How did she get there so quickly, so quietly? Watching her, he's not sure if he should fear her or not. She's a small woman, perhaps in her early twenties, petite to the point of looking nearly emaciated, but she has an ethereal quality he doesn't yet trust.

"We're locked in?" he asks.

"Yeah, they didn't mention that shit to you, did they?" She rolls her ice-blue eyes. "Guess they don't want you leaving whenever you want, getting into trouble or bringing trouble back here."

"Who—"

"I'm Rita." She offers a theatrical wave.

"Stringer," he says. "Joseph Stringer."

"Well, *Joseph*, don't freak on the doors. Not much you can do about it. Could bust them out, I guess, but that's a definite ticket to nowhere, dude." Rita removes a small Zippo from her pocket and flips it open with a quick snap of her wrist. "And I don't know about you, but I got purpose, a reason for being here, you know? Besides, it's full-tilt boogie crazy out there right now."

"It's always crazy out there."

"Even worse these days, haven't you heard? There's a group of killers on the loose." Rita's eyes go wide, as if this news excites her. "For real murderers in the city, they go for the homeless…and other people too."

Stringer cautiously takes a step closer to her. "Somebody's killing homeless people?"

"And others."

"Why?"

"And not just killing them." Rita ignites the lighter. An enormous flame erupts from it. "Setting them on *fire*."

Flames engulfing him, the agonizing pain, the screams…

"Burning them up," she says, finally leaning in to the inferno and lighting her cigarette before snapping the lighter shut. "Right out there on the street."

"Fire," Stringer mumbles, trying to make sense of all this. "I…"

"You okay?" Rita asks this as if the answer is irrelevant. She is amused regardless. "You're looking a little pale there, Joey."

Stringer looks back at the doors then returns his attention to Rita. "Who are you?" he asks.

She draws hard on her cigarette and exhales a stream of smoke directly at him. "I'm sure living in captivity sucks for you, but it makes this all a lot easier than being on the streets."

"All what easier?" he asks.

Rita just smiles and takes a drag on her cigarette.

After a moment he says, "Why are you here?"

"Gee, Joseph, I guess time will tell." Rita's ironic smile reveals big bright teeth a little large for her mouth. "Want to tell me what *you're* here for?"

Stringer fails to see the humor in all this. He shrugs. "I don't know."

"Right," she says with a wink. "You're incurably innocent."

"I didn't say that, I just…I can't remember. Not everything."

"What do you remember?"

"Not much."

Rita throws her head back and exhales another stream of smoke at the ceiling. "You will."

"There's a man," Stringer says. "An old man, he—"

"The dude on your floor, I know who you mean."

"You've seen him?"

"Yeah, saw him once." She shakes her head. "He tends to leave a fucking impression, know what I mean?"

"What's the matter with him?"

Rita's expression suddenly turns serious. "He's diseased," she says. "Trying to find his way back out of his own Hell, that'd be my guess, but I'm just a girl, what do I know?"

"I don't know what any of that means," Stringer says, but something about the word *diseased* rattles him. "What kind of disease does he have?"

"People come and go here. They stay until it's no longer necessary. You know how it is, Joseph."

"No," he says. "I *don't* know how it is."

"You got any coffee?"

He stares at her.

"Coffee, they gave you some, didn't they?"

"Yes. How did you know? How long have you been here?"

"Time's a little fucked up here, if you haven't noticed. It's hard to keep track. Point is I could really go for some coffee." She takes another quick drag on her cigarette then drops it to the floor and squashes it beneath the toe of her boot. "And since you have some, I figured I'd ask. So what do you say? I sure could use a cup of Joe...Joe."

He stands there awkwardly a moment. "Can I trust you?"

"Oh, I think the question is can I trust *you*?" She gives another big smile. "You know, woman in peril and all that."

"You look like you could handle peril just fine."

"Yeah, I'm little but I'm tough."

"You got nothing to worry about from me," Stringer tells her.

"Then let's go drink some coffee."

"I only got one mug."

"No worries." Rita grabs a large black cloth purse from the step next to her, rummages around inside it a moment, then pulls out a mug identical to Stringer's. "I'm packin'."

Stringer nearly laughs, but instead moves by her and back up the stairs.

With another big smile, Rita jumps to her feet and follows.

CHAPTER 7

OWEN WAS RIGHT. IF ANYTHING, THE snowfall had increased since they'd gone into the hold, and though the moon was high and bright, visibility was virtually nonexistent. Stringer held out Tinker's coat. "Take it."

As Owen pulled the coat on, he and Stringer looked out across the flat expanse of ice and snow just beneath the squalls. The wind gusted as if it were born from the darkness itself, cutting through them like freshly sharpened razors.

"I guess there's worse ways to die," Stringer said.

"Always thought fire was the one. Never wanted to die by fire, figured there couldn't be nothing worse than burning alive."

"There's always worse ways."

"At least in this you just go to sleep like Tink did," Owen said. "Drift off and wake up in Heaven."

Stringer shrugged. He'd never had much use for religion. "You think?"

"Can't be in Hell," Owen said. "We're already there."

"Motherfucker finally froze over, huh? Figures, we're dying of frostbite and the night we land in Hell the goddamn heat's off. We can't catch a break."

Owen managed a smile, or perhaps he was grimacing. Stringer couldn't be sure which. He flipped up the collar on his coat just as another series of violent shivers *throttled him. Once they passed, he motioned to the edge of the ship with his frost-covered chin. "Let's go."*

They crawled over the side and dropped to the snow several feet below. The thin top layer of ice surrounding the hull of the frozen ship cracked and shifted beneath them in places, and the men lay motionless for a moment, weak and in pain.

Stringer watched the night sky, barely visible through the thrashing snow descending upon him like an endless swarm of winged predators, and heard himself ask, "You all right?"

"Christ, man, I'm so tired."

Forcing himself to his hands and feet, Stringer ignored the pain. "Get up. You lay there, you'll fall asleep." He grabbed the front of Owen's coat and yanked the big man into a sitting position. A backhand brought him around. "We got to move. Now!"

Owen blinked, offered a disoriented nod, then got to his feet and looked around, trying to find his bearings in the curtains of snow. "Which way, man? Which way?"

Stringer swayed with the wind, nearly collapsed, but caught himself. He looked up at the ship. The mast stood tall, poking through the storm like a beacon. The direction the ship faced would determine the direction they should now head on foot.

He trudged forward, his feet sinking deeper into the snow before making contact with the thick bottom layer of ice covering the water. "This way!" he said, yelling the words back at Owen so he'd hear him above the deafening wind. "We make one straight rush for it across the ice, you hear me? We don't stop, Owen! Not for nothing! We stop, we die!"

Owen reached over, his hand partially concealed in a ragged glove. "Together."

Stringer took his hand and moved into the tempest, screaming in defiance like an animal charging an enemy, or maybe just a man calling out Death and embracing the cold, the snow, the dark, and all the brutality and evil of this malevolent night.

* * * *

"Oh, hell yeah," Rita says, holding the steaming mug with both hands as she takes another sip of coffee. "Thanks, Joseph."

The sound of her voice snatches him back from the nightmare and returns him to the apartment.

"Funny," she says, looking around. "Every apartment in this building is identical. And I mean *identical.*"

He watches her from the far side of the kitchen table. Leaned against the counter drinking her coffee, she looks every bit the lost soul that's wandered in from the storm. Stringer wonders if he looks that way to her.

"What?" Rita asks, noticing he's staring.

"I think I…I think I'm starting to remember things."

"Like what?"

He looks away, unsure if he should tell her. "I was on a ship. It got caught in the ice, in the storm, and I was with two other men, my...they were my friends."

"What were you, a sailor or something?"

"No, I—"

"Maybe you were a fisherman. My dad was a fisherman."

"I never did that either. I don't even think I've ever been on a ship. It's like it's a dream but I...somehow...I know it's real." Stringer rubs his eyes, tries to think. "I remember being homeless. I mean, I—I don't *remember* it exactly, but I know I was. I was here, in the city. But I have these memories of being on a goddamn *ship*. There's a terrible storm, and we're trapped out on the ice."

"Huh." Rita sips her coffee. "Anything else?"

Flashes explode in his mind in a rush—the bloody knife slashing Tink's leg, cutting away the chewy chunk of cold flesh, the feel of it in his mouth, the taste, the texture, the coppery warm blood—and then it's all gone as quickly as it arrived.

Stringer winces and shakes his head. "No," he lies. "Just that I have these memories—or at least I think they're memories—of fire. But they told me there was no fire. They said I was hit by a car and got a concussion and that's why everything's all jumbled. So they can't be memories."

"Wait a minute. You were homeless and remember *fire?*"

"Didn't I just tell you it can't be a memory? Didn't you hear what I said?""Holy shit," Rita says, pushing away from the counter. "You're not one of them, are you?"

"What do you mean?"

"Are you one of the ones doing it?" A strange, barely noticeable smile scurries across her lips. "Setting the homeless, among others, on fire?"

"Jesus Christ, of course not," Stringer snaps. "You think I'm some sort of sick fucking maniac?"

"You never know, Joseph." Rita sips more coffee.

"I know."

"Okay, cool your jets, we're just yappin'." She looks into her mug, as if the answers might be floating in her coffee. "But maybe whoever's offing people in the city aren't bad or maniacs or whatever. Maybe there's a purpose to what they're doing, a good one."

The look Joseph gives her leaves no doubt that he disagrees with this.

"Okay, whatever. But you said you remember, or *think* you remember, fire."

"Yeah, only it was a hit-and-run. Mrs. Milken said there was no fire."

"Who the fuck is Mrs. Milken?"

"The woman that brought me here."

"A woman brought you here? Interesting."

"Why is it interesting? Tell me what you know."

"Well, for starters, how do you know she's telling you the truth?"

"Why would she lie? Besides, if I was burned I'd be in a unit somewhere."

"Good point." Rita walks over toward the window, looks out. "Unless this is all some sort of illusion."

"Illusion?"

"Like, what if we *think* we're here, okay? But we're really somewhere else?"

He sighs, his patience waning. "I got no idea what you're talking about."

She looks over at him. "Sounds kinda badass cool, though, right?"

Stringer rubs his eyes again, hoping to ward off the headache settling in behind them. "Rita, why are you in this building?"

She returns her attention to the window, takes another sip from her mug, and then hugs herself with her free hand. "It's always so goddamn cold in here," she says. "Makes sense, I guess, but I thought coffee might help. It did a little, but it doesn't last, you know?"

Stringer does know. He can't kick the cold either.

"So," Rita says with a sigh, "do you want to fuck me?"

She could not have startled him more had she slapped him full in the face.

"I'm sorry… *What?*"

Rita turns from the window, places her mug on the table. "Do you want to fuck me, Joseph? I mean, I figured you probably would. I can put the wig on if that helps, or are you not there yet? Regardless, it's all going to end the same way. There's nowhere else to go. All you can do is sit here and think. And dream. And remember things you'd rather not but can't forget forever."

"Jesus Christ, it's like you're speaking a foreign language. What are you talking about? Why do you act like you know things I don't but should?"

"You'll get there. And we'll be waiting."

"What the fuck does that mean?" He feels panic rising within him. "In the bathroom down the hall there's a tile missing from the wall. Somebody scratched HELP ME into the sheetrock."

"That's freaky. Doesn't exactly surprise me, though, everybody here needs help." Rita moves around the table, approaches him cautiously. "Do you want to help me, Joseph?" She places a hand on his chest. "Want *me* to help *you?*"

"Rita, what is this place?"

"It's been a long time for you, hasn't it?"

Stringer tries to fight it, but she's right. It's been a very long time since a woman has touched him, since he's touched a woman, and despite his efforts to resist her, his body reacts.

Rita leans in closer, brushes her lips against his ear. "Fuck me," she whispers. "Fuck me, Joseph."

Suddenly she's in his arms and their lips meet. As her tongue finds his, he lifts her up so she can wrap her legs around him. They nearly fall but Stringer catches his balance then spins and staggers toward the bed.

In a tangle, they collapse together onto the cheap mattress.

Just beyond the lone window, the light begins to fade and the snowstorm grows worse, all of it—and them—reflected in the eyes of those long dead and watching silently from the darkest corner of the room.

CHAPTER 8

TRAPPED IN THE HEART OF THE *storm, time lost all meaning. They could have been lumbering along the ice for hours or only a few seconds, Stringer could no longer be sure. What he did know was that the physical exertion had made things worse. His lungs ached and throbbed with each breath, his heart hammered the walls of his chest with such ferocity it frightened him, and his eyes burned to the point that he could only open them for a brief glimpse before they began to tear and close on their own. The sensation in his limbs was all but gone, and on more than one occasion since they'd started out he'd had to look back to make certain Owen was still with him, their hands clutching each other like lost children. His face was tender and raw, but most of the pain had shifted behind his eyes and beneath his skull. His brain was falling asleep, he knew it, and soon his legs would give out. Fear was all that kept him going, because he knew if he fell, it was over. He would never be able to get up, and Owen would more than likely stagger off into the storm without even realizing he'd been lost. The big man hobbled behind him silently, his cracked lips hanging open, his tears frozen to his beard. Maybe—*

They ran into something and pitched forward.

Stringer managed to catch his balance before he fell, but Owen hurtled past and crashed to the ground. Stringer pawed the snow and tears from his eyes, and for a brief instant was able to make out a sharp incline.

They'd run right into it. He looked up in an attempt to see what might lie at the summit, but the snow was blowing too thick. "Owen!" His throat was so sore he couldn't be sure if his voice was still with him. He leaned closer to the ground, saw his friend, and collapsed facedown against the incline.

Stringer grabbed the back of Owen's coat, felt the flesh on his knuckles split as he rolled him onto his back and buckled against him. They lay together in the snow for a moment, neither certain the other was still breathing or even alive. Stringer's fingers were so stiff and numb he was only able to move a couple of them, but he slapped Owen's face with what little might he had. "Don't go to sleep. Stay—stay awake!"

"Help me, man. I can't—Stringer, I can't see!"

"Get up, goddamn it!" Stringer felt the rage boiling in him again, and somehow found the strength to force himself to his feet. "Don't you die on me, you fuck!"

The big man's eyes fluttered and he reached a hand out at the snow as if he were trying to catch the flakes in his palm. "Can't see," he said again. "I...I can't...I can't see."

Stringer screamed and staggered around in an off-balance pirouette. There seemed no end or beginning to the ice and snow. Think, *he told himself.*

They'd made it as far as the incline. The incline...

They couldn't stop now. If they could make it over the rise they might have a chance. Something was there, beyond the incline, not so far away, but Stringer couldn't remember what. The incline led to... What did it lead to?

What the fuck *did it lead to?*

Or was he only hallucinating now, placing trust in a slowly dying mind? All there was beyond that incline was more ice and snow. They were at the mercy of the elements, and at this point the ship was too far behind them to return to, provided they could even find it again in this mess.

No, *he thought,* keep moving.

"We got to get over this rise, you hear me? It's where the water ends! It's where the water meets land!"

Owen's eyes were open again, but whatever they were looking at was reserved for those who had one foot in this world and one in the next. His blistered face was covered in ice crystals, and his arm was still extended, hand out, palm upturned, reaching for help.

Help that would never arrive...

* * * *

The city is quiet, heavy snow has locked it down, frozen it as still as the ice that coats the sidewalks and streets. Along the sides of buildings, running across the rooftops and coating windows, the ice grows stronger, holding the city motionless, squeezing the life from it slowly, gradually, as heavy cloud cover hides the sun and ushers in the beginnings of premature darkness. But this is a false darkness. A lie…

In bed and staring at the cracks in the plaster ceiling, Stringer is slick with perspiration, yet the cold remains. Right down to his bones, it lingers. Rita is next to him, the sheet and blanket covering her. She opens her eyes, searches his for something he does not understand and is certain he could not provide even if he did. Their sex was frantic, nearly brutal in its intensity, but these moments Stringer values more, this quiet time of simply being, experienced as only two people who have just made love can.

"You look so sad," Rita whispers, as if fearful someone else might hear.

"I'm remembering," Stringer tells her, his eyes still gazing at the ceiling.

Rita snuggles closer, rests first a hand and then her head on his chest. Her fingers gently caress the thin line of dark hair that runs from his chest to his navel. "What are you remembering, Joseph?"

Wind rocks the building. It shifts and moans against the assault, and then goes quiet. The wind reminds him not of the icy cold variety in his dreams, or even those just beyond the window, but warmer winds…hot winds blowing from somewhere…else. Winds of fire…

Stringer forces his mind to memories of another place and time, ones that exist so very long ago he cannot be sure if they're truly his own. Unlike the nightmares, they don't frighten him. Instead—these flashes of another, earlier life make him want to cry.

"What are you remembering?" she asks a second time.

"When I was a child," he says, the words catching in his throat.

"Were you happy?"

The ceiling blurs through his tears. "No."

"Tell me about it."

He closes his eyes and gently shakes his head no.

Rita lifts her head, rests her chin on his chest. As her eyes settle on him, she notices a tear running the length of his cheek. "Why are you crying?" she asks, wiping the tear away with her thumb.

Stringer sees himself as a child, eight or nine, watching other kids ride their bikes along a tree-lined street and wishing he had one too. But his foster parents, two in a string of many, don't care about things like that. He is there to be abused and to bring them money, nothing more. It is all he's ever known since his mother left him, but he can barely remember his real parents.

"My life has always been shit," he says.

"Sometimes it's not our fault. Doesn't change things, but it's true."

His bottom lip trembles uncontrollably. The vision fades as the child he once was vanishes into darkness. "I grew up in a Catholic orphanage until I was in elementary school. Then I went into the foster care program. Lived with so many people I lost track. I always knew I was different...damaged, I guess...and I fought as hard as I could to fit in, to be...normal. It just never stuck, so I took off from my last foster home right after high school. I wound up broke, on the street and alone, I..."

"What happened?"

"I survived as best I could."

"That's what we all do."

He knows she's right, but he can't figure out why his life is different. Something tells him she may know, but everything she says is cryptic and strange. Why does she expect him to understand if he can't remember?

"But that was a long time ago," Rita adds, resting her cheek on his chest again as wet snow spits against the window. "So why are you thinking about when you were a boy, Joseph?"

"I...don't know."

"Is that why you're crying, because you're remembering?"

Where is that innocent, wide-eyed little boy? So full of life and love and carefree happiness, where has he gone? Did he ever really exist?

He's dead, Stringer thinks. *That little boy is dead.*

Wiping his face, he rolls away from her and to the side of the bed. His feet on the floor, he leans into his hands and rubs his eyes, fighting the tears until they stop, until he has pushed the emotion back down deep enough where it can no longer hurt him.

"I'm not crying," he says defiantly.

"Who were you?" Rita asks. "Before, when you were still with your real parents?"

"I don't know."

"Are you sure?"

"There's not much I'm sure of right now."

"But it is coming back, isn't it?"

Stringer nods. "It feels like I'm falling through this darkness, and I can't seem to stop."

"That's because you're still falling, Joseph."

Stringer looks back over his shoulder at her. She has now gotten up onto all fours and is looking at him the way a jungle cat sizes up its prey. He wants to respond, but he can think of nothing to say, so he just stares at her, helpless.

Nude, she crawls closer, her startling blue eyes suddenly wild with gleeful violence. "*You're still falling!*"

He vaults backwards, away from her, and crashes to the floor. As he scrambles to his feet and stumbles away, he slams into the table, then spins around and looks back.

Rita is sitting on the bed, looking baffled. "What the hell, dude?"

Her eyes have returned to normal. "Why did you sleep with me?" he asks.

"I have my own way of doing things. The way I see it, sex and violence aren't always so different. The rest is just the way it's got to be. I love dogs, for example. But if one's rabid, if it's sick and violent and can't be helped or cured, then I'd kill it however I had to."

Stringer has had it with her bullshit. "Would you fuck it first?"

"Well, that's gross as shit and definitely not my jam." She gives him a coy look. "But I might pet him. Let him know I cared but have to do what has to be done. The dog would be diseased, after all."

"That word again." Shaking, he backs away to the counter, and realizing he too is nude, gathers his clothes from the floor. "You keep using that word."

"It's important."

"To who?"

"Both of us."

"Look, something's happening to me," he says, dressing quickly. "Something's wrong, something's...something's *wrong*."

"Of course there's something wrong, look where you are."

"Where am I, Rita? What is this place?"

She reaches to the floor next to the bed, comes back with her cigarettes and a lighter. "You're a strange cat, Joseph." She rolls the cigarette into the corner of her mouth, leaves it there. "Very strange...but then I guess most are."

His head pounding, he feels like he's coming out of his skin, as if he's shedding it like some great awful snake. "I need to get out of here. I need a drink. I need to get high."

"All you've got is coffee and cigarettes."

"I'll break the goddamn doors if I have to."

Looking thoroughly unimpressed, Rita draws on her cigarette and exhales through her nose. "And go where? Have you looked outside? We got a bona fide blizzard going on out there, Joey."

Stringer stands before her, dressed but with nowhere to go. "Tell me what this place is. Please. *Please*, Rita. Where am I? What's happening to me? Tell me what you know."

Lying back, Rita spreads her legs a bit, so he can see her. She smokes her cigarette a while but doesn't answer, watching him with those heavily made-up eyes. "What makes you think I know anything more than you do?"

"Don't you?"

"Come back to bed, Joseph." She smiles. Slowly, seductively, the smoke curls around her like restless ghosts. "You need to sleep."

"I'm getting out." He makes his way to the door. "I changed my mind, I—I don't want to be here anymore."

"Can't change your mind," Rita says. "Once you're here, this is where you stay. Until…"

"Until what?"

"Until it's time to go. And it's not time to go. Not yet."

"What's happening to me?"

Rita takes a deep drag on her cigarette, holds the smoke a moment. "You'll know when it's time. The cold, it'll still be there, right down to the bone like always. But you'll feel those winds, Joseph, those warm winds blowing."

"How do you know that?"

"Because you've been dreaming about those winds…those warm and frightening winds…"

Stringer can't get a full breath. His head spinning, he falls back against the door, one hand searching for the knob. "Yes."

"That's when you'll know it's time, Joseph. Because you know what those winds bring, don't you? You know what they mean."

He can see it in his mind, the fire—the horrible flames—engulfing him.

With screams he knows are his own tearing through his head, Stringer yanks the door open, stumbles out into the hallway, and runs for the stairs.

Before he reaches the second-floor landing, Stringer freezes.

The hideous old man is there waiting for him, gangly and nude and contorted, his eyes crazed. He cackles with laughter, the cruel and evil laughter of the damned.

As it echoes along the staircase and into the hallway, the old man grins, then vaults up the stairs.

It is the last thing Stringer remembers.

CHAPTER 9

STRINGER KNEW ALL ALONG THAT STAYING with the ship was the easier move. There was nothing out here for them, nothing in all this desolation except each other. Remaining on the ship was certain death, but it would've been quicker. They could've just given up, in the empty hull, gone to sleep and never woken up. But Stringer was not only a survivor, he was a fighter. Always had been, and when things got this desperate, it didn't much matter to him what a man had to do to make it. Owen didn't know how lucky he was to run from that ship. Had they stayed, Stringer would not have been able to control himself much longer in such a confined space. He'd been around long enough to know better, long enough to know that in this kind of weather, in this kind of place, all bets were off. Stringer realized early on into the night that despite the massive risk to his own life, he'd eventually have to make a run for it. This was their third night in the hull of that dead ship, they couldn't endure much more either way, and he was damned if he was just going to lie down and die like Tinker had.

If I go, I go swinging, he thought.

And even now, though the fight within him was dwindling away like the flames from a slowly fading fire, a few sparks still remained.

Stringer dropped to his knees, tore Owen's coat open, and took him in his arms. "You sleep now," he whispered in the big man's ear. "It's okay to sleep."

I can't fight it anymore.

Summoning all the strength he had left, Stringer plunged the knife into Owen's belly until his thumb struck wet flesh. He'd buried the blade clear up to the handle. With the knife gripped in both hands, Stringer stood up, dragging the blade with him and tearing Owen's abdomen straight up to the sternum.

As he died, Owen tried to scream, but managed only a gurgling groan.

Gutted, the body released its innards along with what little heat remained within it. Stringer leaned his face close, felt the burst of warmth embrace him like a phantom before quickly vanishing, swallowed by the cold and lost in a swirl of snow. The intestines had tumbled free from the cavity and now quivered about in his lap like a mass of bloody eels. Bathed in the tepid blood, Stringer pulled the knife free and began ripping from the bone whatever meat he could find.

* * * *

Lying in the street, Stringer sees an old church materialize through the whirlwind of snow. Still as statues, hands folded in prayer before them, nuns in black habits stand on the granite steps. He reaches for them, for the salvation he mistakenly believes they still represent. It is then that he sees empty raw sockets where their eyes had once been, and frozen streams of dark blood painting their pale, dead faces. As he begins to weep, the nuns turn their backs to him, and in unison slowly ascend the steps.

Stringer drops his face down into the snow, knowing there is nothing he can do to stop this. He will die in the street, alone and unforgiven.

And then he feels hands on his back. Someone is shaking him, and above the howl of a brutal winter wind, a voice calls his name.

"Joseph!"

The storm recedes…

"Joseph, wake up!"

The face that comes to him is Rita's. Hovering over him in bed, she shakes his shoulders a final time. "Jesus, dude. Wake up now."

He squirms away from her, realizes he is still nude in bed. Cold, he's so cold. "No." Still a bit groggy, he reaches for the blankets. "I…"

"That must've been one doozy of a nightmare," she says, sighing and falling back into bed next to him. "You were screaming like a banshee."

Owen's face…both shocked and relieved…the blood…his guts spilling…

In torment, Stringer shakes his head. He wants those thoughts out of his mind, away from him like the horrible and repellent things they are.

It's the truth, Joseph.

"No!" He looks around like the madman he's sure he's become.

Face it. Face the truth, Joseph. Face the truth about what you did.

"Stop," he says, hands to his head. "Make it stop!"

Face the truth about what you are.

"Hey," Rita says, arching an eyebrow. "It's over, take it easy."

What you've always been...

Is he really awake this time? Stringer looks around. He's in the apartment. Has he ever left, or was that part of his nightmare?

"I'm...I'm awake?"

"Yes."

"Just now," he mumbles, "I was on the stairs, I..."

"It was a dream."

And then he remembers her eyes—Rita's eyes—how they changed and turned black, and how she'd spoken with the voice of a demon.

Stringer moves away and out of bed, putting distance between them. "Who the hell are you?"

"Not this again." Rita rolls her eyes and reaches to the floor for her cigarettes. "And thanks for taking the blanket. Not like I'm freezing my hoo-ha off or anything."

"I left before. I left...I...I was going to get out."

"You were asleep. You've been asleep this whole time."

He looks to the floor. His clothes are where he left them. Still shaken, he tosses the blanket and top sheet back onto the bed then gathers his clothes and begins to dress.

Rita adjusts the blankets, kicks them out so they cover her nude body, then props herself up a bit and lights a cigarette.

A headache fires through Stringer's head.

Puffing away, Rita watches him dress through the vines of smoke the way a scientist studies a lab rat, but says nothing more.

Icy particles of snow tick against the window.

Once dressed, Stringer begins to pace. "I gotta get out of here, Rita."

"And go where?"

"Just...*out*..."

"You need a drink, don't you?"

Through his shame, he nods.

"Are you a drug addict, too?"

"Once, I...not anymore, it's just the booze now."

"Oh, it's not just the booze, Joseph. It's important to be honest. Alcohol is only one of your addictions, isn't it?" She smokes her cigarette, her eyes still on him. "You've been on the street for decades. Been a lot of struggles, hasn't it?"

Stringer looks out the window. It's caked with wet snow and the corners have already iced over, but from what little he can see the storm has only gotten worse. He closes his eyes and is greeted by flashes of what was once his life so very long ago. They flicker through his mind like an old, poorly spliced film slithering through a dying projector. A mother…a father…a strange home…

"I'm remembering now," he tells her.

"That's good."

Stringer's no longer so sure.

"You talk in your sleep," Rita says. "You kept saying *Owen*…and *Tinker*."

The sound of their names stings like a slap to the face. Memories of his former life crumble away like dust to reveal more flashes, this time of that horrible night in the storm, on the ship, on the ice.

Blood…so much goddamn blood…

"They were…" Stringer struggles to get the words out. "…I knew them."

"What happened to them?" Rita asks with a wry smile.

He looks away. "They died."

Rita adjusts her position in bed, hiking the blanket a bit higher over her breasts, and then takes a drag on her cigarette. "Tell me about that."

Wincing, Stringer again begins to pace. Like some caged animal, he moves back and forth, his rage barely contained. "They were a couple guys I ran into out there," he says. "We were…"

"Friends, you said."

"Not really, but…I guess that's what they thought."

He remembers a small apartment in a big and scary old building, and how he would sit and play while his mother watched him. Sometimes he would sit in his father's office and play with his toys while his father talked on the phone. Their names elude him, but his mother's face drifts through his mind in shadow. *All those years ago*, he thinks. *Why can't I remember the rest?*

A twinge of pain sears his temple.

Stringer bows his head, closes his eyes again and this time thinks of his father. The memory of him frightens him and nearly buckles Stringer's knees.

He hasn't thought of his father in a very long time. He loved him, as he did his mother. But his father scared him, too.

His rage becomes crippling sorrow.

"You're remembering again, aren't you?" Rita asks.

"It's been years," he says. "I'm trying."

Rita smokes her cigarette and stares at him, expression oddly blank.

"The truth can change a person."

He looks at her, trying to gauge her.

"Only sometimes," she continues, "it doesn't change them so much as it *reveals* them. Sometimes it shows who they really are, who they always were."

"What would you know about it? *How* do you know about it?" Stringer glares at her. "I'm not asking again. Who the hell are you?"

"I'm Rita." She smiles. "Who the hell are *you*?"

"I'm leaving," he says, heading for the door. "I'm getting out. I don't want to be here anymore, I—I'll take my chances out in that storm. Lived through them before and I can do it again."

"Are you sure about that?"

"Watch me."

"You can't run, Joseph. Not from yourself."

"You'd be surprised what I can do."

"Not really," Rita says with a shrug. She flicks a long gray ash from her cigarette onto the floor then takes another hard drag. "Hey, good luck though. I'll see you again. Wouldn't want to miss the big finale, right, Joseph?"

Stringer yanks open the apartment door. He looks back at her, and scowling, slips out, slamming the door behind him.

Even before he reaches the stairs, he hears Rita's quiet laughter bleeding into the hallway behind him.

CHAPTER 10

THE INCLINE WAS STEEPER THAN HE *expected, and gaining a solid foothold on the slick surface was nearly impossible. Despite being stronger for having eaten, twice he had scrambled several feet up only to lose his grip and slide flat on his belly, limbs flailing for purchase, back into the heavier snow below. On both occasions he landed within inches of Owen's remains. Even the blood had frozen in place now, hanging in crimson icicles from the wounds while the rest had congealed into a solid but slowly vanishing puddle surrounding him. With each passing moment the storm concealed more evidence, until Owen's body was little more than a lump against a snowbank.*

Stringer lay on his stomach while his body buckled, his bowels seized, and he vomited bile and human flesh. Slowly, he pushed himself forward, determined to scale the incline a third and final time. Digging his hands and feet into the fresh blankets of snow, he ignored the wind and cold and darkness, and pulled himself up one short lurch at a time. He fully expected to lose his grip and slide back down into Owen's lap, but this time his efforts paid off, and he managed to crawl up and over the apex.

The ground was again flat, but now he could see something in the distance, something through the snow. It was faint and very far away from the looks, but there was *definitely something there.*

Had his mind finally snapped, or was whatever remained of his soul giving way and being shown a glimpse of things to come? Was it lights?

Follow the light. Go toward the light. *Isn't that what people always said?*

Stringer could no longer feel his body, but he had the sensation of rising and knew he had either somehow managed to get to his feet or was floating off to his death. Either way, he squinted through the snowflakes and tried to focus on the strange lights in the distance. He felt himself stumbling forward, and suddenly the terrain was different.

It wasn't until he fell that he realized he had, in fact, been walking. The ground here was different than the frozen water below. It was mostly snow here too, but a bit deeper in places and considerably shallower in others. Here it blew about into enormous drifts to his right and left, while at the center it was—

Wait, *he thought,* I'm in the middle of a street!

Could that be possible?

Stringer pushed onward, struggling to see the lights in the high-rise buildings through the darkness and snow flurries, blinking stars in a manmade skyline. But then a heavy burst of snow engulfed him and down he went again, sprawled out in the street as the lights and all else disappeared into the whiteout.

Only the terrible cold remained.

And the faint beating of what Stringer could only hope was his heart.

* * * *

This time when Stringer descends the stairs, he reaches the ground floor to find the doors open. Wind blows snow into the foyer, and an icy chill cuts right through him. Beyond the doors, thick walls of violent snow form a barrier that destroys any hope of visibility. Waves of arctic air continue to assault him, dragging him back until he remembers what it was like to be lost in such weather and entirely at its mercy.

Despite his fear, Stringer steps down from the staircase and onto the snow-covered floor. At least an inch has already accumulated, and it's only getting worse. It is not lost on him that there is nowhere to go now, yet the doors are not only unlocked, but thrown open. Whoever—*what*ever—is behind this is playing with him, as if for sport, Stringer is certain of it. They're taunting and tormenting him on purpose, and the more he remembers, the more these thoughts and visions rip apart whatever remains of his rational mind.

Defiantly, Stringer forces himself out through the doors.

The icy snow hurts on contact, so he tucks chin to chest and struggles slowly through the storm until he reaches the street. Visibility is still bad but better here, so using an arm to block the wind and snow as best he can, Stringer continues on until he reaches the sidewalk on the other side of the street.

The city is deserted and locked down in the blizzard, but several lights remain on, including the neon sign to a liquor store a block and a half away. Stringer can make out enough of it to use it as a beacon, so he leans into the wind and pushes his way along the street.

Once he reaches the store he tries the door, and to his surprise, finds it unlocked. The wind makes it more difficult than it should, but he manages to force the door open wide enough for him to slip inside.

The storm quiets immediately. Stringer wipes snow and ice from his face and looks around. The place appears empty. He moves down an aisle, finds the whiskey and grabs a bottle from the shelf. As he returns to the front of the store and the counter area, he sees there is still no one working the register.

He assumes whoever works here must either be busy or hunkered down in the stockroom, as no employee would leave the store unlocked.

"Hello?" Stringer calls out. "Is anyone here?"

His voice fills the silence, and then just the sounds of the storm remain, barely audible beyond the heavy door. His breath still labored from his trek through the snow, Stringer thinks maybe he'll stay a while. Apparently he's alone here, which is just as well since he has no money to pay for the bottle anyway. Besides, it's quiet here and warmer than the building. He can drink in peace and have as much as he wants. There's even food. Only snacks, of course, but more than enough to sustain him until the storm passes.

Suddenly something in the corner of Stringer's eye catches his attention, a strange bending of light just above him and to his left. He looks up and finds the culprit, a large circular security mirror mounted over the counter that bends and warps his appearance.

Just as Stringer realizes it's simply his own reflection that distracted him, something else comes slowly into focus at the farthest reaches of the mirror.

A man is standing in the shadows, a small red light blinking from an old camcorder on his shoulder.

The bottle drops from Stringer's hand and shatters as it hits the floor. He jumps back and out of the way, furiously spinning around to confront the man filming him.

But there is no man.

Stumbling, he puts a hand on the counter and catches his balance, then looks to the mirror a second time. Nothing...

Stringer focuses on the broken glass and spilled whiskey on the floor around his feet. With fear and shame strangling him, he angrily stomps back to the whiskey aisle and plucks another bottle from the shelf.

This time he opens it and brings it to his mouth.

"Do not be merciful, but be just..."

He pulls the bottle from his lips and staggers away from the shelf, eyes darting about the store. Like last time, the voice was not in his head. He heard those cryptic words being spoken. Goddamn it, he *heard* them.

"Who's there?" He walks cautiously toward the door he assumes leads to the stockroom. "Who are you? Where—goddamn it—*where* are you?"

The wind answers, nothing more.

Stringer replaces the cap on the whiskey and shifts his grip to a position lower on the neck of the bottle. It's heavy and full, and can do serious damage should he wield it like a weapon, which he is prepared to do if necessary.

Carefully placing his free hand against the stockroom door, he gives it a slight push. It opens to reveal a large room with a cement floor, the walls lined with freezers and stacks of boxes containing various beers, wines, and liquors.

"Come out!" Stringer says. "Show yourself, goddamn it!"

No one responds, nothing moves.

He waits, holds the door open. His eyes search as much of the stockroom as possible from his position, but there are shadows and corners he cannot see. Someone could easily be hiding undetected.

It could also be a trap, Stringer thinks.

After a few seconds he takes his hand from the door. As it swings closed he heads for the front counter. If any money's been left behind in the register, he wants it. Enough cash can get him out of this city, maybe even afford him a bus or train ticket like a regular person.

I can head south, he tells himself, *like I should've before all this began.*

Standing behind the counter, Stringer opens the bottle of whiskey then takes a long pull. It feels warm going down, and he instantly feels sated, a scratch finally itched. But the satisfaction is short-lived and replaced almost immediately with sorrow and regret.

He places the bottle on the counter and tries to distract himself from his shame by focusing on the register and how to get it open. Although he hits several keys, none release the drawer. Frustrated, Stringer grabs the bottle and takes another swig. His shame becomes anger.

"You're nothing but a goddamn loser," he mumbles.

"You're a murderer, a disease."

As a chill rushes up his spine, Stringer's head snaps in the direction of the stockroom, where he's sure the voice came from. He holds the bottle down against the side of his leg and slides out from behind the counter.

It's then that he sees something seeping out from beneath the stockroom door.

Blood…

A river of it flows toward him, slowly spreading and fanning out into a giant puddle across the floor.

"You're a disease, Stringer, a disease that must be eradicated."

His mind splitting, he backs away. He knows the voice coming from behind the door. It's different from the others he's heard.

This one he recognizes.

"Owen?"

"You're a monster and a degenerate, a sick animal that needs to be put down…"

The stockroom door slowly opens a few inches, and from inside, large thick fingers slither out and curl around its edge. The skin is bruised and split from frostbite. Stringer knows those fingers, and recognizes them.

"I saw you die," Stringer says just above a whisper. "You're dead."

"We're all dead, Stringer."

The world blurs as his eyes fill with tears. "I'm alive!"

As the door pushes wider still, he drops the bottle and runs for the exit. Slamming into the door with his shoulder, he explodes back out onto the street and into the storm, nearly slipping on the ice before catching his balance. Arms flailing, he bolts in the direction of his apartment.

He's nearly there when he sees something in the middle of the street.

Sliding to a halt, Stringer quickly looks behind him for the first time.

Nothing but swirling snow…

Turning back, he tries to get a better look at whatever is sitting in the street before him, but it isn't until he's gradually circled around to the front of it that he realizes it's a little boy sitting in the snow.

Even with the icy snow stabbing at his face and eyes, Stringer knows who it is. He knows that face, those eyes.

His face…his eyes…

The little boy holds a small toy truck in his hands, one of the wheels missing. He looks up, seems to notice Stringer for the first time, but seems completely unaffected by both the storm and his presence.

"*No,*" Stringer says, emotions throttling him but his voice lost in the wind. "Don't—not—not this, please, not this!"

Expressionless, his child self raises a tiny hand and points at something over Stringer's shoulder.

He looks back, and through the snow makes out the outline of the building. On the third floor, one window facing the street is filled with dull yellow light. Within that lighted square, three stories up and burning through the swirling snow, is a man looking down at him.

It's his apartment. Someone's in his apartment besides Rita.

Stringer turns to question the boy he once was, but he's gone.

When he returns his attention to the window, he realizes what he's looking at—*who* he's looking at—and a sharp pain stabs his temple again and again, as if someone is slamming the blade of a knife through his head.

As his knees buckle and the world turns upside down, tumbling like some amusement park ride gone mad, everything slams to darkness.

The man in the window is him.

CHAPTER 11

NO ONE EVER DREAMED OF GROWING up and becoming a monster. No child ever gazed off into space on a rainy day and fantasized about one day living on the street like a wild dog, alone but for those other forgotten and discarded souls who inhabited the corners and alleys and parks and roadways.

No one ever dreamed of being a horrible creature somewhere between human and ghoul, drinking and washing in the blood of their victims and eating their flesh in order to sate a ravenous diseased hunger that never leaves.

No one ever dreamed of being evil and horrible and vile.

No one sane...

So in those rare times when there was room to dream, to forget the harsh realities of an existence like his and pretend things were different, Stringer preferred to think of himself as an adventurer, an explorer too full of restless courage to ever settle down and live a mundane, traditional life.

But those were lies, and no one knew that better than he did.

So while in this nameless city, where he continued a search that he had pursued his entire life, he hooked up with two other road dogs who knew nothing of his past or true nature. Despite the weather reports warning of the worst blizzard in years, he'd opted to stay one more winter night. They could've followed the same route most did, the same one they had for so many other harsh winters, escaping the north for the warmer southern regions this time of year—and eventually would have—but Owen was so sure another night wouldn't be all that bad, and Stringer knew this presented him with an opportunity. Surely the shelters or one of the homeless camps throughout the city would have room for the likes of them, and come morning they'd hop a train out of town and begin the trek south. But they'd been turned away at the shelters, all were full, and being unfamiliar with this particular city, they had yet to locate any camps when the blizzard struck.

They'd heard rumblings about some crazies that were supposedly on the loose, but it was hard to tell if that was true or just stories. Every town and city had their dark tales, urban legends, and ghost stories. Most were just that. But why take chances? And besides, in that weather, no man could've lasted more than a couple hours exposed out on the street anyway.

No man.

Cold, hungry, and trapped in the storm, Stringer, Owen, and Tinker started across the frozen bay abutting the city in the hopes of reaching the suburbs on the other side, miles in the distance. But they'd not gotten far when the storm forced them to take refuge in the bowels of a monument a mile or so offshore, a reproduction of a small fishing vessel—a memorial dedicated to local fishermen lost at sea over the years—and a day and a half later they were still attempting to survive within its granite hold while the blizzard raged on.

And Stringer's hunger became unbearable.

When Tinker froze to death, it became apparent that no one would live through this ordeal unless certain risks were taken, certain sacrifices made. If there was one thing Stringer took pride in after all his years on the street, it was staying alive. Regardless of what he was faced with, he did whatever was necessary to survive.

Until now…

"Not here," Stringer gasped, crawling along the frozen pavement. "Not in the street. Please—please, not in the street."

In the distance, he could see the silhouette of a large building across from where he'd fallen. Through the sprays of snow, a church with wide granite steps emerged. A seaman's church that catered to sailors and their families, it overlooked the ocean and the monument from which Stringer had come. A church for other lost souls, for those the sea and the elements had taken from this world, a church for those they left behind and for those yet to come.

He knew this church. He had been here before.

He begged the storm, but his legs would no longer work. Paralyzed and sobbing only feet from the curb and church steps beyond, Stringer dropped his face to the pavement, into the snow. As he neared his final breath, he forced his head up so that he could see the statue of the Blessed Virgin on the church steps, her head bowed as if she'd been expecting him and had already begun to pray. But as the snow blew past, during one pocket of clarity, Stringer noticed other forms standing on the steps as well. Were they nuns?

Just like all those years before...

"Help me," he said, hopeful they'd heard him. "Please...help me."

Before his eyes slid shut, though he still wasn't certain what they were, the dark forms descended the steps, moving silently in his direction through the snow.

* * * *

As the snow and darkness lift, Stringer sees a little boy sitting on the floor of a small cluttered office playing with his toys, waiting for his father, an older and disagreeable man sitting behind an old desk barking orders into a telephone.

He recognizes it immediately as a room in the building where he lived his earliest years as a child. The man behind the desk is his father. And the little boy is him.

Stringer feels the emotion catch in the base of his throat as tears fall from his eyes. He wants nothing more than to reach out and touch this place and time, to feel it and hold it, warm and safe. *Here should be rescue*, he thinks. But it is anything but. Although his father is a stern and powerful and frightening man, Stringer loved him desperately as a small child, and strove for his attention, acceptance, and approval.

As the little boy looks up at a plaque on the wall behind his father's desk, Stringer looks too. And there he has the answer to the words he's heard in his waking nightmares.

The plaque reads:

*"Do not be merciful, but be just, for mercy is bestowed upon the
guilty criminal, while justice is all that the innocent man requires."*
—Khalil Gibran

Stringer feels something cold and bone-like touch his arm.

Mrs. Milken stands next to him, her fingers curled around his wrist like the spindly legs of a huge spider. "Mr. Stringer," she says, "it's time."

He looks back to the office, but it's gone, replaced by the wall of his apartment, the snowstorm raging just beyond the window.

"I don't understand." Stringer quickly wipes away his tears, embarrassed.

"You need to come with me."

She releases his wrist, and for this Stringer is grateful. "Where's Rita?"

Mrs. Milken's face shows no emotion whatsoever. "We'll see her soon."

"What's happening?"

"This way," she says, moving toward the door.

Reluctantly, Stringer follows her out into the hallway and to the head of the stairwell. The old man is standing just outside his apartment door, looking like some gangly demon and as full of madness as ever.

"It's all right," Mrs. Milken says, sensing Stringer's uneasiness.

The old man steps closer, his crazed eyes locked on Stringer.

And in that horrible moment, Stringer realizes who this man is.

"No," he whispers, his legs quivering.

Ignoring the man, Mrs. Milken descends the stairs.

As the old man grins and reaches for Stringer with his gnarled, claw-like fingers, Stringer hurries down the stairs too, only looking back once he reaches the second floor.

The old man glares at him, then lurches away down the hallway and out of sight, howling like a mortally wounded animal.

"Mrs. Milken—"

"He's beyond help," she says, continuing to the ground floor.

Stringer trails her to the ground floor and then down a short jog of a hall that leads to a door to the right of the exit. She hesitates long enough to retrieve a large ring of keys from her purse. Selecting a key, she slides it into the lock and turns. The door unlocks with a loud clunk.

As she opens the door, a burst of musty air greets them.

Stringer looks closer. It's an entrance, but not the way he'd imagined.

The door opens directly into an old elevator.

Of course, he thinks. *What else would it be in such a hellish place?*

Mrs. Milken pulls back the chain grate and then slides open the elevator door. There appears to be enough room for one, perhaps two people, but no more. She steps away then motions with her hand for him to enter.

"What is this?" Stringer asks.

"It's time," she tells him. "This is our process, Mr. Stringer."

He shudders. This bizarre old elevator is the last place he wants to be. Stringer knows there's only one way for that elevator to go, and that's straight down. But to where? What awaits him down there: a basement, some sort of secret underground cavern, or something far worse?

"Mr. Stringer," she says, motioning again. "It's *time*."

Horrible pains shoot through his legs like razors slicing his flesh. "My legs—they—I'm having terrible pains in them and I've been—I've been collapsing a lot, passing out, and when I come to things aren't right, they—"

"This is the way out." Mrs. Milken purses her thin lips. "The *only* way out."

"Where will it take me?" he asks.

"To the truth," she says with a sigh of impatience. "It's time to stop seeing through the eyes of a lie."

Stringer steps into the elevator. "Who are you? Who are you really?"

Mrs. Milken is the last thing he sees, as he's still awaiting an answer when the doors close, plunging him into sudden darkness.

Slowly, the elevator begins its descent.

CHAPTER 12

THE SOUND OF WATER ECHOES IN his ears. Not running water, but a more natural sound, like waves softly lapping a nearby shore, or the runoff from a mountain stream trickling into an otherwise quiet cavern. The darkness recedes and his eyes open, but sight comes gradually, painfully, the skin flaking and crackling as he blinks. Blood, ice, or both slide in freezing tracks along either side of his face.

Someone is standing above him. He realizes he is no longer in the elevator, but lying down. He is lying down and someone is standing above him, looking down, watching. Stringer swallows, then gags and coughs, the sound ricocheting along the walls of wherever he's been taken. He struggles to bring the person above him into better focus. Squinting, he sees the face of an older man, his skin weathered and cracked like leather exposed to the sun for long periods of time. A black knit hat covers his head.

"Where am I?" Stringer asks in a weak voice.

"Where do you think you are?"

"The elevator, I—"

"There is no elevator here."

"But I—Mrs. Milken, she—"

"Who?"

Stringer desperately searches his tattered memories. "A church, I—I remember a church in the storm."

"You think you're in a church?"

"I don't know, I…"

The man's eyes stare at him dully. "That church is for seamen, the living as well as those already long dead. That church, just like the monument in the bay, is for men and women trying to earn an honest living, trying to feed their families. And those who died trying…"

Stringer tries to move but he doesn't have the strength.

"You found the monument to them," the man explains. "It gave you shelter in the storm, and you desecrated it. Now you expect sanctuary in the same church, is that it?"

"I don't know what the fuck you're talking about. I didn't desecrate a—"

"We know what you did in the hold. We know what you did in the snow. We know what you are. It's what we do. Your kind isn't the only one that hunts."

"I did what I had to do to survive," Stringer says, biting his bottom lip in the hopes of preventing it from trembling. "You got no right to judge me, who the hell are you?"

The man stares at him. "We're the ones that eradicate the disease that is you and your kind."

The crazies—it's true—they—

"Where am I?" Stringer asks again.

"Under the ice…in the ocean…on the street…in the snow, does it matter?"

Stringer looks down, sees that he is covered with a blanket, and it is wet. His body is still numb. "I can't feel my legs."

"Frostbite," the man says. "They couldn't be saved."

"What—I—what did you say?"

"They could not be saved."

"No, I—God no, it can't be, I—my legs!"

The man motions to his right.

Stringer's head lolls to the side, and he sees another man who looks much like the first, only a bit younger, standing there grinning at him. In his hands like trophies are Stringer's bloody legs.

They have been severed just above the knee.

Others emerge from the shadows and form a circle around Stringer.

"You took my legs," he whispers. "You—you took my legs."

"The storm took them."

Tears stream like ice water across Stringer's cheeks. "You took my fucking legs! You had no right to—"

"We have every right!"

"This blanket," Stringer gasps. "It's soaking wet and smells and I'm so cold, I—get it off me."

Just beyond the old man, Stringer sees a lone figure standing in the shadows. Slowly, Rita steps into the sparse light, an unlit cigarette dangling from her lips. She smiles, but it's a cold smile, one of contempt and hatred.

"Rita," he says, trying to reach for her but unable to move. "Rita, help me."

She laughs lightly, shakes her head, takes a drag on her cigarette then steps closer still. "Not gonna happen, Joey."

The others all hold their hands out, as if warming them over a fire. A wood match seems to materialize from nowhere into the older man's hand. He strikes it against the table Stringer is lying on. As it ignites, he holds it over Stringer and leans closer.

"The blanket is soaked in gasoline, Joseph."

"Is this Hell?" Stringer gasps.

The old man seems amused. "Almost…"

"Am I dead?"

"Not quite," he says.

"You—this—must be real, I can see your breath. All of you, I see your breath, I—I can *feel* you shivering all around me."

"Of course you can." The man holds the lighted match higher.

"Please don't do this."

"Is it mercy you seek?"

"Yes!"

"Do not be merciful, but be just," the man says. "For mercy is bestowed upon the guilty criminal, while justice—"

"Is all the innocent man requires," Stringer finishes for him.

"Which you are not," he says. "And why you're begging not for justice, but mercy."

"Please, take the match away. I'm sorry for what I've done, I—don't burn me, I—please—I swear I'll make it right, I—I swear on my soul, I'll—"

"Have you forgotten already?" the man asks.

An eye on Stringer, Rita leans in, lights her cigarette from the match flame and gives him a maniacal wink.

No, Stringer thinks, *God help me, I remember it all.*

"Your soul is no longer your own."

As the man drops the match, Stringer is lost in a sudden explosion of flames and the deafening shriek of his own excruciating screams.

CHAPTER 13

AS THE SUN BREAKS OVER THE horizon, shining on the city and surrounding bay, daylight brings with it a renewed sense of hope. The blizzard has passed and the city is slowly awakening from its hibernation. What was deadly for the last three days has now turned delicate and beautiful, as warming rays of sunshine reflect off a vista of virgin ice and snow. Gradually the world begins to thaw. Snowplows and other vehicles crowd the avenues while pedestrians bundled in their best winter clothes hurry from corner to corner, from coffee shops to offices, from still-chilly morning air to the warmth and shelter and security of their workplaces, embracing the solace and routine of their daily lives.

If anyone notices the body on the side of the road, it doesn't seem to faze them in the least. No one stops or looks down for more than a quick, distasteful glance. But the body *is* there, slumped in the gutter in front of Saint Mary's, a huddled mass of frozen flesh burned beyond recognition.

This gruesome display is nothing new, however. In blizzard conditions or on extremely cold winter nights, the homeless have been known to set fire to themselves, and even each other.

And then of course there are the rumors of a band of killers in the city, a clan that has been murdering its victims in a horrifically vicious and cruel manner. Often dismembering them and then setting them on fire, they leave the brutalized remains in the street like trash.

Regardless, later on either someone will eventually report the presence of the scorched body or the authorities will notice and call in a wagon to haul it away, so no one gives it much thought or pays any particular attention. Despite the weather, there is no hurry.

Time is a strange thing here.

PART TWO

WE DIE FOR LOVE

"We each die countless little deaths on our way to the last. We die out of shame as humiliation. We perish from despair. And, of course, we die for love."

—Clive Barker

CHAPTER 14

THROUGH THE FLAMES—THE FIRE—COMES a rush, a burst, and then everything peels and pops and blisters, burns away like film to reveal what lies beneath.

Drifting through the fog of an impossibly dark night, she weeps in agony, knowing the others are close. They've found her, but it doesn't matter now.

And then suddenly she's engulfed by an odd sensation. It's like being in an elevator, but she cannot figure out if it's going up or down. Whatever it's doing, it's moving, first at a slow crawl and then with alarming speed until—

Pain—godawful pain! God help me! God, please make it stop!

It sears through her stomach and radiates up into her chest. She opens her robe, lifts her hospital gown, and cringes when she sees the long, deep cut on her belly, a network of thick black stitches the only thing holding her together.

Terror mixes with confusion, and she can't remember how she came to this or what is happening to her. Despite the sun shining through a pair of large arched windows, it's terribly cold in the room. She can see snow on the ground, and a radio hums softly somewhere nearby, an announcer's voice droning on and on about heavy downfall and gusty winds paralyzing the city for an entire day and night.

And then there's a news story, something about murders, but she can't quite make it out. She focuses instead on the rumble of snowplows down on the street, and the water steadily gushing from the gutters along the roof.

She lowers her gown as another wave of pain rips through her.

A voice sounds, eerie and detached, but unmistakably human.

"Carla?"

She realizes then that a nurse is standing just a few feet from her. She looks at her with confusion, and uncertainty bordering on horror. In a voice soft and weak she asks, "Where am I?"

"You're in the hospital, Carla." The nurse is all dark hair and eyes, with a shockingly pale face and bony hands. "An attendant brought you out here. We thought you might enjoy some sunshine."

"Who are you?"

"My name is Agatha. I've been in charge of caring for you here."

"The pain, I—"

"Yes, I'm sure it's quite severe. We'll get you your medication."

Carla remembers snow…the cold…a dark highway…

"I came here during the storm?"

Something on the side of the road…there was…something…

"You've been here long before any storm." The woman's gaze flickers to a window. "The snow's melting, and according to the weather forecast warmer air is on the way. Despite the pain you're experiencing, you're actually healing quite well. In a few weeks, should all continue to go well, and assuming you get the go-ahead from the doctors, you'll be released to a halfway house."

"A halfway house?" she asks.

"Yes, for women like you." The nurse frowns. "You signed the forms, don't you remember?"

"No, I—what's happened to me?"

"The state police found you. You apparently lost control of your car at a high rate of speed and hit a guardrail. The car was destroyed, and you suffered a rather severe gash to your abdomen. You were only barely conscious when they found you."

"I saw something. On the road, I…I saw something."

The nurse arches a penciled-on eyebrow. "And what was that?"

"I can't remember but…it was…"

"Yes, well—"

In a sudden rush, she forgets the dark highway as something else comes to her. "My child!"

"It's important you remain calm."

"Where is he, where's—"

Agatha stares at her blankly. "You can discuss that later with the doctors."

Vague memories of speeding through the night in an old car flicker through Carla's mind. "But where *is* he?"

The nurse purses her lips. "Not here."

Emotion wells in her. "Won't I get to see him?"

"I don't know, Carla. You're still under observation for now."

"I don't understand, what—"

"Do you remember crashing the car?"

"Not really, no. It's just mostly flashes."

"I see."

Pulsating light blinks in her head, the distant sounds of metal twisting and plastic and glass shattering echo in her ears and then…silence.

Carla looks to her, trembling. "I…"

"You easily could've killed yourself."

"It was an accident, I—I would never deliberately—"

"In fact, it's a minor miracle you weren't killed. At this point, the baby might be better off…elsewhere."

"There's been some mistake. He needs to be with me. I'm his mother!"

The nurse offers a coldly patronizing smile. "As I say, if all goes well, in a few weeks you'll be transferred to a housing unit, a halfway house. They'll work with you and help get you back on your feet."

"I don't care about that," Carla snaps, her head reeling. "I want my son!"

"Give this all some time. For now, try to enjoy the morning."

"*Enjoy the morning?* Where is my child?" Carla looks around, but she's so weak she can barely hold herself upright. "I want to talk to someone. This is a mistake. Let me talk to someone in charge."

"Becoming upset will only make the pain worse."

"You listen to me. I demand to—"

Pain slashes across her abdomen and up into her chest with such force it takes her breath away, and she nearly passes out.

"There," the nurse says. "You see what you've done to yourself?"

But all Carla sees is darkness closing in around her like the slowly lowered lid of a coffin.

CHAPTER 15

WHEN SHE COMES AWAKE, CARLA FINDS herself in a wheelchair, a duffel bag resting on her lap. Agatha is still with her. Perhaps she's never left.

"What is this?" Carla asks, feeling the weight of the bag on her legs.

"Medication and other necessities like clean underwear, toothpaste, a toothbrush, soap." She lowers her eyes. "Once you get to the halfway house, they'll give you a small apartment."

"I'm leaving already? But you said it would be a few weeks."

"It's been several weeks, Carla."

How is this possible? She can only remember just awakening here. It feels as though she's just met Agatha a few moments ago.

"The medication can sometimes make time seem rather *fluid*," Agatha tells her. "It's not unusual to experience rather severe *gaps*, as it were."

Carla looks at her helplessly. "Will I see you again?"

"No."

"What about my baby? Won't anyone tell me where—"

"I'm sure you'll be given more information at the appropriate time."

"But why can't—"

"Good luck to you." She pats her hand, but it is mechanical and without compassion. "Follow the rules. That's why they exist, do you understand? Stick to the rules, do what you're supposed to do and how you're supposed to do it and perhaps you'll see the light."

"What does that mean?"

"One cannot see the light until one embraces the dark."

Before Carla can question her further, a young man dressed in a blue nurse's uniform appears. He smiles warmly then drapes a woolen pea coat over her shoulders. "Ready, dear?"

"I want to see my baby," she says.

He wheels her down a gloomy corridor. "They said you're healing up nicely. Plenty of good food and rest, I bet you'll be fine in no time."

"What is happening to me?" she asks in a hushed tone.

Rather than answer, he stops in front of an elevator, presses the down arrow. When the door opens, he wheels her into what looks like a waiting area, through a set of automatic doors, and finally out to a small parking lot. A small blue bus with the word RESIDENTS etched on its side awaits them.

The back door is open.

The man gently lifts her, helps her up a ramp, and holds her arms as he lowers her into a seat. As he places the duffel bag at her side, he says, "Bye, Carla. Take your meds and follow the rules, you hear?"

He's gone and the door shuts.

The driver, a stocky older man, smiles at her in the rearview, and then begins to drive away, out of the empty lot and onto a highway, where fog spirals from tar and a lone man stands on the side of the road draped in shadows. His neatly combed silver hair is what she notices first, and then his eyes black and death-like, as he raises a camcorder, balances it on his shoulder and aims it right at her.

When she rubs her eyes and looks again, the man is gone, lost in a whirlwind of nightmarish visions and disjointed memories.

Carla doesn't want to sleep, but they've medicated her and she can't help it. The soft bumping and the sound of the engine lull her closer, and as darkness cradles her in its wings, she dreams.

CHAPTER 16

THE MAN IS SEATED BEHIND A desk, his eyes cold. His is older, has a gangly frame and is bald but for a horseshoe of gray hair. He looks at the woman before him as though he can see right through her. And maybe he can, because she can tell he's met many just like her, confused, scared, with scattered memories of the past, fragments that come and go but always seem to remain just beyond their grasp. He opens a file, flips through it, and then speaks with a precise and detached voice, "Carla, my name is Lou Dante. I'm in charge here." He glances at the paper before him once more then continues to speak to her without making eye contact. "Looks like you've been through quite an ordeal. According to your records, you're single, have no fixed address, no job, and your parents are both deceased."

She nods.

"Due to your circumstances, your mental state, and the fact that you not only tested positive for cocaine but had a blood alcohol level well beyond the legal limit at the time you crashed your car, since you had no prior criminal record, you were offered the chance to come here instead, which you agreed to. All the forms have been signed, so here you are, and here you'll stay until we deem you ready to return to the world as a normal, functioning, contributing member of society. As you should've been told by now, this is a halfway house, of sorts."

His emphasis on *of sorts* is somewhat disturbing.

"I don't remember a lot about the crash," she mumbles. "All I know is that my son needs to be with me."

"Your son?" the man asks. He finally makes eye contact, but his gaze is cold, almost cruel. "I don't see anything here about a child. But if what you say is true, he's either still in the hospital or was sent to foster care while you were recovering. If he exists we'll find him, but—"

"Of course he exists, he—"

"Carla, you were drunk when the car crashed, and if you had a kid with you the odds that you'll get him back—at least for the foreseeable future—are almost nonexistent, okay? Just being honest with you, there's really no sense soft-pedaling it."

"I just made a mistake, I—"

"About this place," he interrupts, slapping closed the file. "We offer shelter and hot meals. We have rules here. Rules you'll be expected to follow without question or argument. Remember, you easily could've done jail time, and the only reason you aren't behind bars right now is because you're here instead. With one phone call I can have your ass sitting in a cell in a matter of hours, understood?"

Carla nods.

"I didn't quite hear you there."

"Yes," she says softly. "I understand."

"Excellent. Now, long as you do what's expected and don't cause any problems, you'll do just fine. Frankly, nobody cares about the people that come here. So long as we shelter and feed girls like you, and keep you from further burdening the system, they'd just as soon forget all about you. Out of sight, out of mind, know what I mean?"

"Yes," Carla says, though she doesn't understand any of this.

"I'll be here to help you through all this, don't worry." Lou stands and makes his way around his desk to her side. "I'll take you to your room. It's not much, but you'll be safe here. Long as you earn your keep, know what I mean?"

There's something wrong with this man, Carla can sense it, something not right about what he's telling her. And she's certain if he asks her one more time if she knows what he means she's going to lose whatever's left of her mind.

He places a hand on her shoulder. His grip is powerful. "Stand up."

She obliges, surprised at her ability to do so. She's still very weak, and rather lightheaded, but the pain in her abdomen is gone.

As the man's eyes move over Carla's body, a sly smile emerges. "You're awfully thin," he says, "but you'll do. We can fatten you up a little."

"How long was I in the hospital?" she asks, trying to mask her discomfort.

He leans over and lightly kisses her cheek. "Don't worry about that," he says, running his hand across her back. "You're *here* now."

"What are you doing?" she asks, forcing a quick, joyless, nervous laugh.

"Remember what I told you." He pulls her closer against him, his sour breath hot against the side of her face. "Don't cause trouble and everything's going to be okay."

She slams shut her eyes. *God help me*, she thinks.

But Carla knows God is nowhere near this place.

Only night without end…dark and unforgiving…

CHAPTER 17

CARLA STANDS BEFORE HER BEDROOM WINDOW. Like every morning, there's no memory of leaving her bed, though the covers are turned down and the sheets are wrinkled. Only dreams remain, fragments of a man making love to her.

"Neither of us is the same now," he breathlessly whispers in her ear. *"Those days are gone forever."*

She closes her eyes and sees herself sitting in a small theater, a black and white film flickering on a huge screen before her. A face fills the screen…her face. Slowly, the camera pulls back and she realizes she's naked, legs parted as a man crosses a darkened room. He kneels before her, forces her legs wider apart, then touches her. Gently, the lovemaking begins.

For an instant, she sees another man, a shadowy figure standing beside them. A camcorder rests on his shoulder, the tip of a cigarette dangling from his lips glowing in the darkness.

Maybe it's just a dream, but deep down it feels more like a memory. She sighs, opens her eyes and looks down at the street below. The city is beautiful after a storm, especially in the morning when seabirds swoop down over the ocean then soar up to a clear, blue sky. People move along the street, their faces flushed from winter's chill, smoky tendrils floating from their mouths.

When that beauty fades, the remnants of vile acts reemerge, yet few seem to notice. But some mornings, Carla does. She sees the remains. Her eyes take in traces of smoke rising from a mangled pile of ruined clothes, singed hair, and burnt skin.

Won't be long before a wagon arrives to take the poor soul to a mass grave, a desolate place located on an island three miles from the city—a place where ocean waves crash against rocky ledges. It's always the same, and yet this time—this body, or what's left of it, is oddly familiar somehow.

"Did I know you?" she whispers, her breath fogging the window.

A rustling sounds behind her.

"Carla, you have a client tonight. I hung the outfit you need to wear in your closet. Don't forget your makeup."

She turns, gazes at her unmade bed a moment then she shifts her focus to a dark corner of her bedroom. Lou leans against the wall, his dark eyes fixed on her, a cigarette clenched between his teeth.

"Can't you ever knock?" she says, her voice trembling with anger. "I wish you wouldn't just barge in on me."

"Watch that pretty little mouth of yours, bitch." He smirks cruelly. "I'll do whatever I want whenever I want, got to keep you on your toes. And besides, I'm not around that much anymore. I thought you'd be glad to see me." Lou takes a long drag then releases smoke through his pale lips. It floats away, vanishing like a ghost. "But if you're going to be a cunt, I can—"

"I want to see my son. You're keeping him from me. I want my baby."

"Well, be a good girl and I'll make sure he's with you later on." Lou smiles, but there is no affection in it; instead, it's a smile of superiority and control, of dominance. "I took him from you because you were bad. Don't you remember?"

Carla's head begins to ache as images flash, revealing a mournful place where depraved acts occurred, dark eyes taking her in, shifting to the little boy beside her—specters that drift in and out of her consciousness. And a question, one that has haunted her for a long time—years—decades.

An ethereal voice asks as it has many times before. "The baby, is he mine?"

CHAPTER 18

IT IS EARLY AFTERNOON WHEN THE sun begins to melt snow from the rooftop. It trickles into the building's gutters as the wind disturbs, then carries away, ashes from a nearby fire that burned while Carla slept. The body's gone now, but a rusty stain remains behind on the pavement. The entire city is stained with the blood of those taken in the night. Here, in this building, it's always so cold, no matter how bright the sun shines through the windows, no matter how hot the radiators hiss.

Soft cooing blends with those sounds; her baby is asleep in his hand-me-down crib. Carla tries to remember if Lou brought him back. Or was he here all along? Did she dream that she rocked him to sleep, holding him tight, humming softly? Tenderly kissing him on the cheek, her eyes fill with tears. No, this man, the one who visits without warning, is not the caring guy that she once knew—the ghost who weaves in and out of memory—a lover she betrayed.

Carla runs a hand over her forehead. "Everything's off," she says softly. "Time…it's like it's out of sync."

She gazes at her son. He's had a bath, because the smell of soap lingers in the air. Damp ringlets cling to his forehead and thick, dark lashes flutter as he dreams.

What does her baby dream about? Is it a better life, in a place away from this musty apartment, where mice don't scurry across the floor and roaches don't come out when the lights go off? Are her son's dreams of a grassy yard and a new bed, with a beautiful bedspread and plush pillows? Is it warm there? Is there no danger? Is there only love?

Something's going on in the alley beneath the window. Shouts and glass breaking, then a woman screams.

The child stirs. His eyes open, he smiles, almost wickedly as the woman in the alley whimpers and metal scraping pavement echoes up from the street below.

The boy turns, and then drifts back to sleep.

"I promise I'll get you out of here, baby."

"Mommy…"

With a ghostly timbre, a child's voice, a lost *thing* tumbling through time.

"I'm here, I…"

The child that had been sleeping soundly in his crib is gone. Now there is only emptiness, gloom, and the smell of flowers.

Lightheaded, Carla pinches the bridge of her nose, hoping to lessen the sudden headache behind her eyes.

Darkness…

* * * *

Her mother had an Italian library table, and in summer she lined it with flowers from her garden. On this day, the remains of what was once a beautiful bouquet sat in a vase on that same table, the petals brown and the leaves scattered about the floor. Chris brought her the flowers, his hands trembling as he placed them in her arms.

"I get lonely," he said. "But I never do shit like this."

"What kind of shit?" she giggled.

"I don't know, be all romantic, I guess. But from the minute I saw you it was like I knew you. You're so pretty, and there's something in your eyes. I knew we belonged together."

Carla had good memories of him. He wasn't like other men. She didn't force herself to drift away when he lay on top of her. His breath didn't stink of liquor, and his hands were warm when he touched her. A fisherman, he came to her whenever he returned home from a trip, slim and handsome, with tousled hair and brown eyes. Tattoos of ravens and Celtic circles adorned his arms.

"Got every one of them when I had too much to drink," he told her.

She touched a dead rose and the petal tumbled to her feet.

Just like me, *she thought.* Dead…dying…no longer beautiful…

She remembered Chris the day he left. With sweat beads dotting his forehead, his body still slick with sweat from their lovemaking, and his eyes rimmed with red and boring into her, he'd whispered, "The baby, is he mine?"

"No," she told him, bowing her head in guilt. "You went away and while you were gone things got bad, they got hard and I...I was all alone, I..."

His face that day, Carla would never forget it. She could've lied to him, he would've never known, but she wanted to be truthful. If they were ever to have a real life together, he had to know the truth. She'd fallen, as she had so many times before in life. It was a mistake, but she was alone, without family or any close friends, in a cruel and unforgiving city. The liquor, the drugs, the bad decisions, they had plagued her for most of her life. And now, they had cost her the only man she ever truly loved.

* * * *

The words and memories fade away. Carla's throat tightens and the words freeze, as cold and heartless as the city at night.

When she dreams of Chris, of making love with him, she sees a figure standing above them in the shadows. A man, his face obscured, a camcorder hoisted on his shoulder. He watches them, his tongue slowly licking his lips. And then the bed erupts into flames.

She and Chris don't seem to notice. Their lovemaking only intensifies.

Until darkness takes it all back, and everything goes still.

"Chris," she whispers. "You've been away so long. Come back to me."

Sometimes she tells herself maybe his boat was lost at sea, but she knows deep down that it's more likely he found another girl, someone younger perhaps, and without a child. Someone without the same problems she has had for so long. But he'd always told her none of that mattered, and sometimes she allows herself to believe he still cares— wherever he is—and that maybe his promises weren't just cheap talk. She'd been hurt before, but she knew now how horribly she'd hurt him. She'd been alone and desperate and afraid, drinking too much and doing drugs and making bad decisions, and it had cost her. She knows that now, and yet, she sometimes still hopes for his return, for his forgiveness.

She misses Chris. She misses him a lot. But she isn't sure she's worthy of him, or his forgiveness. And yet, does she truly deserve...*this*?

There is no bathroom in her apartment, only one per floor. As her head clears, she realizes that's where she is, though she has no memory of having come here. Slowly she sinks to the floor and leans against the toilet. A single tile is missing, pieces of it lie on the floor, as if it's recently fallen off and shattered. Carefully, Carla selects the biggest, sharpest shard and slowly carves two words into the space left behind by the fallen tile.

HELP ME.

She hears the phone ringing down the hallway. It jolts her and brings her back. Struggling to her feet, she tosses aside the piece of tile then hurries back to her apartment.

Once there she runs for the phone and answers it. "Chris?"

"It's Lou, you stupid shit." Music can be heard from wherever he's calling from, a strip joint most likely. The tinny music, the laughter, the cursing, it's all amplified over the phone and disguised as background noise.

"Sorry," she says meekly.

Carla envisions Lou seated at a bar, talking on a phone brought to him by a sultry bartender, a topless dancer gyrating a few feet away. She remembers dancing too, but not like that. It was innocent. Wasn't it? It was with Chris, the man she loved. It was real. It was right. And now that memory is all she has.

"Fucking airhead," Lou snaps. "Don't you remember? You got a customer. I'm sending him up in about an hour, so get your ass ready."

"What about dinner? I haven't eaten."

"Mommy?"

"My son hasn't eaten either, he—"

"We'll take care of that later. Right now, you get your shit together."

She turns, sees the child curled up on the couch, thumb in his mouth and a little foot tucked between tattered pillows. Reeling, Carla almost passes out but catches her balance by leaning against the table. Time…it…there's something wrong. He was in a crib, just a baby, only moments before, how could…how in God's name could her son be three years old?

"Hey! You hear me?"

The sound of Lou's voice startles her. "Yes," Carla says. "I hear you."

She also hears something moving just outside the apartment door. Most of the apartments are empty on her floor, and no one comes and goes from the building except for a handful of people. The john's check in and out with Lou, none ever come and go without his prior knowledge.

"He's not already here, is he?" she asks.

"Jesus Christ, are you even listening to me? What'd I just say? I just told you I'm sending him up there in about an hour."

"Sorry," she mutters. "I'll be ready."

Carla hangs up the phone, and then glances at her reflection in an oval mirror hanging over her bureau. She's a pretty girl with wind-swept auburn hair, a milky-white complexion, and a petite figure. Has she always been so pale?

"Chris," she whispers.

Once, when she first came here, Lou warned her about remembering and placing any stock in the past. Things were different now. *She* was different now. Forget about Chris, forget about the random man she'd slept with that had impregnated her. That was her life before. Now it was all about never getting too close to a john, and never allowing herself to think they cared for her. And absolutely *never* have any feelings for them. It's all business and survival, Lou says, nothing more, nothing less.

But she still thinks of Chris as her salvation, a ticket out of this hell of poverty and prostitution and things far worse. A way out of Hell...

Last time she saw him, even though she knew his heart was broken, he'd told her he was going out on another fishing trip, but he'd be back. "I need to go get all of this out of my system and get my head around what's happened. This guy, the father, do you love him?"

"I love you. I don't even know him. I've never even seen him again."

"I want to take you with me out to the West Coast when I get back. I'll have the money and we can just go. We can start a new life there and forget about all this."

"Do you really mean it? You forgive me?"

"By the time I get back, this'll all be in the past."

It's been so long now, she's come to grips with the fact that he's never coming back. And yet the idea that he might one day return has kept her going. Now, Carla realizes that if she's truly determined to end this way of life and give her son a better future—a better life than she's had—no one's going to save her but herself.

She can't stay here, can't take this life for too long, or she'll end up like the other women in the building, most she never sees but sometimes hears. Their screams travel up the staircase in the dead of night, riding the late-night breezes through open windows.

Visions of bloody meat erupt across her mind's eye. Red meat, thick with dripping juices, bloody and nearly raw...

Sometimes she hears talking on the stairs, voices fading when elevator doors whoosh open from somewhere in the building. Lou's laughter when the archaic machinery struggles somewhere deep in the bowels of the building. There are always new voices, new laughter in the night...

And then new screams.

The apartment house reeks of filth and sin. It feels ancient, as though it's been here longer than surrounding structures, maybe even longer than the city itself. Sometimes, late at night, Carla swears it feels as if the building itself is alive somehow. And in those moments, she feels like she's been here from the very beginning, a lost soul tumbling through time and space.

She looks at her son. Much as she hates it, for now, Lou and his dark offerings are their only means of survival. "Time to go, baby," she says with a frown.

Carla lifts him from the couch, kisses him on the cheek, and carries him down the hall to Suzie Mitchell's apartment. Suzie is the only other resident she knows, and to a point, trusts.

The full-figured brunette opens the door with a cigarette hanging from her mouth, and a *TV Guide* in her hand. "Got a date, kiddo?"

"Yeah, Lou just called. Would you mind?"

"You know I don't."

"Thanks." She hands him over.

"I remember the days I'd have to leave my little one with a neighbor when a call came from Lou." She runs her fingers through the baby's hair. "Such a long time ago now, it's—it's been such a long time."

"Lou's been around that long?"

"He's aged well, some do. Others not so much, but that's mostly right before it's time for them to go."

Carla checks the hall in both directions. They're alone. "Where do they go, Suzie?"

"Ain't no secrets here, honey," Suzie says with a wink. "The walls are thin. Voices carry. You just got to listen. Lou don't want us to hear too much, that's why he keeps us all dreamy, see? It's why we all sleep so much."

Carla's heart crashes her chest. "Lou, he—"

"He's got you under his thumb, just like the rest of us. But it changes."

"How?" she asks.

"Do what you got to do. Bide your time."

"The others, when they age and leave, are they escaping?"

The expression on Suzie's face is one of sorrow. "Not exactly, but in a way you could say that they're on to…other things."

"What happened to your baby?" She's never asked this before, and a lump forms in her throat before she can get all the words out. She and Suzie have had many conversations, but never about anything too deep, and while Suzie's mentioned having had a child in the past, she's never explained where her daughter is or what became of her.

Suzie winces as if in physical pain. "She's gone on from here. Long time now, she's gone on from here."

"Where is she, Suzie?"

"Some other nest, I guess." She stares at her, and after a moment she slowly shakes her head. "I don't know where."

"Did you say *nest?*"

"You know what I mean."

"No, I don't."

"You will."

"I have to get my son out of here."

"Yeah, well..." Suzie smiles as the baby opens his eyes, snuggles up to her, and then drifts off to sleep again. "We'll be here when you're done, okay?"

"Thanks, I owe you."

"Go get ready, and be careful."

With a nod, she starts back to her apartment.

"Hey, kiddo?"

Carla stops and looks back.

"This won't be forever," Suzie tells her. "Sooner or later we all come out on the other side. One way...or the other..."

CHAPTER 19

THE OUTFIT THAT LOU PROMISED HER is hanging on a hook in her closet. Denim jeans, size five, circa 1970s. A halter top, embroidered at the edges, butterflies, roses. Is that a blood drop on the neck?

And she dresses slowly, dreading the man who waits for her.

Carla doesn't remember going to him, coming to this room where only a twin bed is pushed up against a wall. The floor is hardwood, scratched, and a lightbulb hangs from a chain on the ceiling. The man's around sixty, balding. He's naked, thin, sizing her up as she undresses.

"When you're done stand under the light a minute and let me look at you," he tells her. "You ever do movies? Could swear I saw you in one once. It only lasted about ten minutes or so, but it was a good one. Yeah, that *was* you, wasn't it? Got it on with two guys, right?"

"Never did anything like that," she answers softly.

"Sure, honey." He chuckles and winks at her, as if this is a secret they now share. "I get it."

"Sorry, wasn't me."

"I know it was you. Remember, stand under the light."

Carla pretends she's stripping for Chris, and he's on that bed singing to her, telling her it won't be long before he comes back for her. But when she goes to the man, there is no foreplay, no gentle kisses, just a rough thrust inside her. And it hurts. It always hurts. Just like the first time.

Things escalate quickly, as they often do, and things get rough. Most of the guys that come here are that type to one degree or another, so it's not as if Carla isn't prepared or doesn't know how to handle it, but that does nothing to make it any less unpleasant. Like Lou has always preached, she is there to do things that a lot of wives and girlfriends won't.

"Lie still," he tells her, then touches her, his hands icy even though the furnace rattles and steam floats from the hot radiator. But still, it's cold, colder as he molests her with his bony fingers and nips at her with his sharp teeth.

"Take it easy," she says. Her heart pounds, this man could kill her with those hands if he wants to.

"What did you say?"

Carla pretends to smile and act as if she's enjoying herself. "Just take it easy, okay? Don't have to be so rough, we'll have fun."

His eyes flair with anger, and without warning, he slaps her across the face. Once, and then again, backhanding her viciously.

For a split-second, a flash like an explosion of flames erupts before her eyes, and the john becomes the shadow man she's seen in her dreams, the strange man with the camcorder, watching…recording…

"It's extra for that shit," Carla says, her lip bloody and already swelling.

He slaps her again and with a sinister laugh says, "I got money, I'll pay whatever it is. You just do what the fuck you're told."

When it's over, he pays her more than the usual. "A real pleasure, Carla," he says. "This was my last stop before I go away. We all got to go away sometime, even you. Don't matter how. Could be old age, cancer, by gun or knife, maybe even fire, but the bottom line is, we *all* got to go."

He gives a quick bow before he leaves her, equal parts formal and comical. But there is nothing funny about this man, or the way he's made her feel.

As Carla lies there, staring at the ceiling, ignoring the pain and trying to compose herself, she hears the elevator sound down the hallway. Lou's voice rises above the mechanical sounds but she can't make out what he's saying.

After a moment, a second voice sounds she recognizes as the john. It sounds as if he's pleading, desperately trying to convince Lou of something.

And then the screams come, as she feared they might.

The bloodcurdling screams of the john, and then...silence.

Alone with her pain and terror, Carla closes her eyes and tries to sleep.

* * * *

She doesn't remember what happens before dinner, just that Suzie brings her a plate. It's the same as always. Red bloody meat barely cooked, and little else. Carla has grown used to it after all this time, and consumes it quickly.

Suzie takes the plate and tosses it into a large garbage bag, one that already appears quite heavy. As she drags it across the floor toward the door, things inside appear to move, as though living creatures reside within it. With a grunt, she finally reaches the door, her ample body moving as if in slow-motion. "Damn thing's heavier than usual tonight," she says.

Once she's maneuvered the bag into the hallway, she leaves it there for someone else to retrieve, then returns with a smile, two droplets of blood staining her chin. "Feeling better now that you had something to eat?" she asks.

Carla wipes her mouth with the back of her hand. "I eat to live."

"Don't we all?" Suzie says with a cackling laugh. "The bastard was hard on you earlier, huh?"

She nods, rubs her bruised lip. "He said he was here on business, staying over at a hotel by the ocean. I think he got into it with Lou after. I heard them in the hallway."

Suzie waves her hand. "Fuck him, let Lou handle the assholes."

"I have to get out of here, Suzie."

Her face grows dark. "It's not as simple as that."

"Can't anyone help?"

"You got to understand something," Suzie says. "People like us and places like this are invisible to the rest of the world. There's us and those that come here, understand? And even when they do see, nobody cares, Carla. Nobody gives a shit. I've always believed this place summons the people it wants and needs. If you're meant to come here or find this place, you do. If not, you walk right by and never even notice. We're just rumors, bedtime stories to scare the kiddies."

"My son, then, I—I don't want him growing up around all this."

With a frown, Suzie nods. "Kiddo, I—"

"He's just a child. He didn't ask for any of this, he doesn't belong here. He's good. Not like the others. Not like us."

"I know, I—"

"I don't want Lou to do to him what he's done to all of us."

Suzie gives Carla's leg a quick reassuring pat. "Get some rest. I'll keep him with me for a couple more hours so you can get yourself together. I'll bring him around in a while and we can talk more then, okay?"

"Suzie, will you help me? Will you help me get him away from here?"

She hesitates at the door. Just beyond, in the hallway, someone has come for the garbage bag. It's being dragged away and sliding along the floor. The sound gradually fades away to silence before Suzie finally answers by silently mouthing the words *I'll try*.

Carla smiles through her tears. It's the best she can hope for.

* * * *

"Am I dreaming or are you really here?" Carla asked.

The shadow next to her bed became Chris. He sat down next to her, smiled and gently stroked her hair. "Shh," he said. "It's me, it's all right now."

"You came back?" she asked, the words catching in the base of her throat. She wanted nothing more than to sit up and put her arms around him, but for some reason she couldn't seem to do it. She was so groggy, as if sleep wouldn't quite let her go. "Is it really you?"

"Yes, it's me."

"How did you find me?"

"Don't worry about it, I'm here, that's what matters."

"Do you know what I am now, what I do?"

"I don't care about any of it. I love you."

"How did you get in here? It's so late."

"I found a way inside the building," he said. "No one knows I'm here, don't worry."

"Lou says he has people by all the doors and guys that watch the building. I've never had the guts to try to get out."

"You don't have to worry about anything tonight," Chris said.

He leaned closer, and Carla saw flowers in his arms. His hair was damp from a light snow falling just outside the window. "I had to see you. I just want to sit with you and talk about the future, our future. But I don't have much time."

"Take us with you, the baby and me," she said, desperately trying again to sit up but failing. It felt as though she'd been drugged. "Chris, get us out of here. Please, you don't know what happens in this place, what they're doing to me and what they'll do to my son."

"Fishing was really good this trip. Got more money than I know what to do with,

we can take it and start over somewhere else. You, me, and the baby, all of us, how does that sound?"

"Lou won't let us leave," she told him, fighting back tears.

"If he tries to stop us, I'll kill the fucker with my bare hands."

"You don't know what Lou is—what—what he's doing to us, he—"

"It doesn't matter. I'm going to take you away, don't you understand?"

"He'll stop you."

Chris kissed her forehead. "That's not true, Carla, I'm taking you and the baby to the west coast with me. You'll never have to see these people again or even think about this life because it'll all be in the past. You never would have ended up here if I hadn't left you. But now you'll never have to do things just to survive ever again. You can do anything you want. You can get a job and work if you want to, or maybe go to school, and I'll make sure you and the baby both have everything you need."

"If that's really true then please get us out of here. I'll go anywhere with you, just get us out before Lou—"

"Don't worry about him."

"Chris," she said, her voice shaking, "he's not..."

"What? He's not what?" He rested his palm against her cheek. "It's all right, Carla, you can tell me."

"He's not..."

Chris smiled, gently stroked her cheek with his thumb. "What?"

"He's not human."

He leaned closer, his face breaking through the shadows, his eyes red as fire, glowing in the darkness. "No kidding, bitch," he growled. "Neither are you."

* * * *

Carla snaps awake to find Lou slapping her in the face again and again, stinging and humiliating. Her lip begins to bleed again, and she tries to squirm away, frantically searching for the light, an escape to her nightmare. But there is no escape. It's just a trade, one horror for another.

"Jesus, you're a fucking idiot," he shouts. "I should kick the shit out of you." He clenches his fist, shows it to her and shakes it in her face. "Ought to beat you to death right here and now, you useless little twat."

Carla knows better than to even ask what she's done. Instead, she just braces herself for the beating to come. Much to her surprise, Lou slowly relaxes his hand and drops it down to his side. "You think you can get over on me? Do you really think you can do that?"

She shakes her head no.

Icy rain pummels the building, streaking the dirty windows, the sound of it blending with soft music playing somewhere in the building.

"Do you really believe the fisherman you knew years before you even got here is coming back for you?"

Carla shrugs, afraid whatever answer she gives will be wrong.

"He's not," Lou says. "He wouldn't know where to find you even if he did."

She doesn't want to believe him, but her heart sinks into her belly and she suddenly fears she might pass out. How does he know these private things that go on in her head? "He was just a boyfriend," she lies.

Lou raises his hands again and steps closer, glaring at her. "Don't you know you can't even dream without me? I'm right there with you every time, Carla. I'm in your head and in your soul, what's left of it anyway. I *own* you. Forever, bitch, for eternity. That's how it fucking works, and if you had a brain in that head of yours you'd understand I'm setting you free, I'm making you whole, you fucking dumbass." He lights a cigarette, exhales a cloud of smoke at her, then holds the orange tip just inches from her face. "And stop asking Suzie to help get you and the kid out of here. Don't you know I'd never let that happen?"

From his nearby crib, the baby smiles up at Lou. His eyes are dark brown like his, and sometimes they have a similar glint she can only describe as evil.

Lou goes to the child, picks him up with surprising care, and rocks him in his arms. "Straighten your shit out, Carla, or you won't ever see him again."

"Don't take him from me," she sobs.

"He's mine, too. Remember that."

She tries to focus on him through her tears. "That's not true."

"First day you came here. We made him. Don't you remember?"

"No, he was already born when I got here, he…"

Lou laughs. It's horrible and evil. "You were pregnant when you got into that car accident," he tells her. "You lost that baby, the one you made when you cheated on that faggot Chris. You and I conceived this kid, Carla. Right here in this building. *This* is his home, *I'm* his father, and he's not going anywhere."

The words tumble away, becoming phantoms in that horrible room. And once more they vanish, like not quite fully formed memories, flashes of a man that loved her despite her infidelity, promises of a home on the beach, flowers in a garden, the kind of life that most take for granted. All of it gone, all of it a dream that never was and now never can be.

"I'm crazy," she mutters. "That's it, isn't it? That's why nothing makes sense and I can't remember things right. I'm crazy."

"Crazy as hell, baby," Lou says, still holding the child and grinning.

"Crazy as motherfucking hell. We all are."

CHAPTER 20

HER SON SITS CROSS-LEGGED ON the floor, a toy truck in his arms, a fragile thing bought at the five and dime, one of its wheels missing.

In the deepest recesses of her mind, Carla considers a misty and distant memory of Lou bringing her son that truck, laughing and cheering him on when he accidentally pulled the wheel off. When did he bring her son back to her? Was it yesterday or this morning?

Time, it seems, lurches out of sequence again.

And the toddler becomes a small baby cooing in a basinet.

Just as quickly, he returns to his three-year-old self, pounding that sad little truck on the hardwood floor.

A man standing at the door and holding flowers smiles. A gentle soul, his eyes are filled with love. He is completely unaware that his life is in danger. She wants so badly for it—him—to be real.

But she knows it's not.

"Things are happening," Lou told her earlier. *"It changes you, and until the change is complete, nothing seems real or right. Everything is haywire and out of sync, and you can't tell the difference sometimes between your dreams and reality. You sleep a lot, but that passes too. Your body is adjusting, becoming, and your mind and soul*

follow, understand?"

Chris fades, flickers like film, and vanishes.

Anger flares deep in Carla's gut. She looks to her son. "Fuck this place," she snarls. "You deserve better. We're leaving tonight."

Her son looks at her, his eyes so much like Lou's.

She throws open her bureau drawers, stashes diapers, snacks, and a couple of fresh outfits for the baby in a duffle bag.

Before she can scoop the child up from the floor, the door opens.

Lou. Behind him, Suzie and several other women, along with three strange men she has never seen before. Their skin is deathly pale and looks as if it's beginning to decay.

"Going someplace?" Lou asks with a smirk.

"I'm taking him out of here," Carla says defiantly, her heart drumming her chest as she grabs her son and holds him tight. "I'm taking him away from you and all of...*this*."

Lou balls his hands into fists but leaves them at his sides. "All of what?"

Before Carla can answer, the child stretches out his arms, fingers wiggling, his eyes fixed on Lou.

"Daddy," he says.

"Good boy." Lou reaches for him. "That's it, come to Daddy."

He coos, and they look at each other with the same dark eyes.

"Don't you touch him," Carla says, backing away. "I swear to God, I'll—"

"There's no God here, Carla."

"Just relax, honey," Suzie says from behind him. "Everything's going to be all right, just don't cause a fuss, okay?"

"Last chance," Lou says in an eerily calm voice. "Hand him over or I'll take him from you. And if I take him, you'll never get him back."

The corridor lights flicker and the women turn in unison, as if programmed to do so. Together, they float away down the hall, vanishing into the dark and leaving Carla alone with Lou and the three men.

"Give me what's mine," Lou says. "*Now*, you little bitch."

"He's not yours," Carla says, spitting the words at him. "Please, Lou, don't do this, please, I—"

"Mercy, is that what you want?"

Tears streaming her face, Carla nods.

"Mercy is for the guilty." He steps deeper into the room. "And you're just as guilty as the rest of us now, aren't you?"

"Please, Lou, don't hurt him."

"Hand him over, or you'll get nothing even close to mercy."

Trembling, she does. There's no other way.

Lou kisses the boy's cheek, tells him tenderly, "Stay by me, buddy." Then he bends, releases him from his arms, and gently places him on the floor next to him. The child clutches the edge of Lou's jacket with his tiny fist, and presses his head against his father's thigh.

Lou slides a hand into his jacket pocket, retrieves a VHS tape, and smiles maniacally at her. Slowly, he hands it to one of the other men.

The man slowly lifts something he's been holding down at his side. A camcorder. He balances it on his shoulder, slides the tape into the side, then snaps it shut. It is the first time she's seen his face clearly, but Carla realizes now who it is. His face is pale, his eyes black, and his silver hair short but thick and neatly styled. He wears a blue blazer, a perfectly pressed white shirt, tailored, cream-colored slacks, and a pair of leather loafers. He smiles at her. It is a filthy, depraved smile. The red RECORD light on the camcorder flicks on, and the man brings an eye to the viewfinder.

"What are you going to do to me?" Carla asks, her gaze returning to Lou.

"Cleanse you, baby. I'm going to make you whole. It's time."

Carla hugs herself. She can't stop shaking.

"It's time to be reborn."

* * * *

Carla comes awake in darkness.

She thinks she hears a man's voice begging for his life, and Lou's sick laughter rising above those pleas, but she can't be sure if it's real or just some lost fragment of a nightmare she was having before regaining consciousness.

It's so dark here she can't be sure where she is, but the smell of cooked meat wafts about from somewhere nearby. She feels around in the darkness but there is only a cement floor and, eventually, a wall and a closed door, nothing more. She crawls around some more but can't find a way out.

Just when she's about to give up, she hears a heavy lock disengaging and the door swings open. Although the shaft of light that enters the small room in which she finds herself is not terribly bright, it hurts her eyes for several seconds until they adjust and she can see.

A silhouette stands in the doorway, places something on the floor before her: a platter with a few scraps of meat sitting in puddles of dark blood.

"Who's there?" she gasps.

"Eat."

Carla knows that voice. "Suzie?"

"You must be hungry. Once you start, it's not like it ever stops."

"Help me."

"Carla, just eat."

And she does. God damn her and them all to Hell, but she does.

Devouring the food greedily, she stuffs it into her mouth, hardly chewing, attempting to quench the perpetual ravenous hunger that plagues her.

"Good," Suzie says. "Don't you feel better now?"

Carla gives a weary nod, her face smeared with grease and blood and tissue. "What have they done to us, Suzie? What the fuck have they done?"

"It'll be better soon."

"What are they going to do to me?"

"He's going to make you stronger, girl. Better. You'll see."

Suzie steps back and away, and partially closes the door, leaving only a minor sliver of light to cut the darkness in the room. "We all went through it just like you are now," she says. "You're almost there, kiddo. Be strong."

"Wait!" Carla screams, reaching for the door.

But it slams shut with a deafening thud, swallowing the last of the light and returning her to darkness.

* * * *

How long has she been here? She's hungry again, but so dreamy and confused and *cold*, so goddamn cold. Certain she heard something, Carla cocks her head and listens, squints at the surrounding darkness.

Against the far wall, a light… It flickers on then off then on again. From over her shoulder, she sees the light coming through a small square hole. It hits the wall before her, projecting images on it like a movie screen.

Though it's in black-and-white, the first image is Carla's face. It fills the wall, and as the camera pulls back, she sees a man is kneeling before her. They're both nude. He touches her face, neck, and breasts, then mounts her, moving slowly at first, and then savagely.

"This stuff gets you hard?" she watches herself ask breathlessly.

The man laughs. "It's you. You're the star of the show."

"Me?"

"Don't you remember?"

Still on her hands and knees, Carla crawls closer to the film playing on the wall. She knows it's her she's watching, but she doesn't remember being with this man. There's been so many, sometimes they all blend one into the next.

A blurry memory pulses across her mind's eye, a dark highway, too much whiskey, dope, and coke…something frightening on the side of the road that shouldn't—can't—be there—but is…a horrible and deadly crash.

"That's what got me here, isn't it? To this life, to guys like you."

Watching and listening to herself, Carla feels like she's floating away.

"Yes," the man answers. "Now come be my movie queen."

The film suddenly stops, plunging Carla back into total darkness. But the sound from the movie continues.

The woman that is her begins to scream.

* * * *

Each night, Suzie brings her a plate of meat. Each night, it gets rarer and bloodier, and each night it becomes easier for Carla to consume. She finds herself wanting it, needing it, and the guilt and horror of it all slowly begins to recede and dissipate. All she thinks about now, all she wants, is to get her child as far away from this madness as possible.

On the last night, Lou brings her dinner.

Tonight he serves her something with the meat. Cradled between two bloody slabs lies a severed finger, veins and chunks of muscle dangling from it.

Lou stands over her, grinning from the shadows. "Go ahead," he says.

Stomach growling, Carla lifts the finger from the platter and quickly bites into it, gnawing greedily with her teeth. In her mind, she's aware of what she's doing, and yet, somehow, it no longer repulses her. Savoring the coppery taste of blood, she continues eating, tearing the flesh from the bone.

When the other meat is devoured and all that remains of the finger is the cleaned bone, Carla tips the plate and drinks the blood. With it running down her chin, she wipes it away with the back of her hand, then licks her hand clean.

Sighing, she tosses the plate toward the partially open door without looking, her head bowed as she feels a horrible stabbing pain in her stomach followed by a surge of power.

Still on her hands and knees, when Carla raises her head, she sees Lou lording over her. Leaned against the wall, one foot propped against it, his expression is one of amusement and triumph. It isn't until he pushes away from the wall and steps closer to the light leaking through the still-open door that Carla realizes her son has been watching from the hallway the entire time.

"You sonofabitch," she whispers, slurring the words, her tongue still thick with blood. "You sick sonofabitch."

The boy picks up the plate she threw, looks at it a moment, then licks a drop of remaining blood from it.

Lou laughs. "Kid's learning his first lessons early."

"Stop it," Carla sobs. "He's just a child, Lou."

"It's all he knows. All he'll ever know."

If it's the last thing I do, Carla thinks, *if I have to die trying, I'm going to get him out of here.*

"Good luck with that," Lou says, and then steps out into the hallway. "See you soon."

He picks the boy up in his arms and slams the door shut with his foot.

Returned to the loneliness of darkness and silence, Carla crawls to the far corner of her cell, draws her knees to her chest, and wraps her arms around her shins. As she rests her chin on her knees, she assures herself this is all nothing more than a sick dream.

CHAPTER 21

ALTHOUGH IT CAME TO HER IN *the form of a nightmare, Carla knew it was really a memory. The day she was sent to this awful place, the day Lou forced himself on her, that's when this really all began. He took far more from her that day than her dignity. He took her soul.*

She'd blocked the memory of that day from her mind, but knew she could no longer wield that kind of power over it. Despite her best efforts, the memories continued to come, flooding from her mind in a rush of violent waves that crashed over and dragged her beneath, drowning her in the depravity and madness, the pure evil of it all.

There were others watching, and the strange silver-haired man with the camcorder, he was there too. Off to the side and filming the whole thing, he whispered things she could not hear while now and then laughing quietly.

"Don't worry about them," Lou whispered. His breath cold and smelling of the grave made her sick to her stomach. "It's just us now, you and me, baby."

As he thrust into her, he arched his back, threw back his head, and opened wide his mouth. Long sharp canines like those of a wolf glistened above her.

And then Lou fell atop her with his full weight, his sweaty body pressing against her, pinning her down as he closed his mouth on her neck.

Pain—piercing, burning—and then a pop and release...

Sucking, he drew from her things far greater and more vital than blood.

As her head lolled to the side, she saw the others watching, smiling with something similar to pride, as the man with the camcorder kept filming, licking his lips and muttering unintelligibly.

When darkness fell over her, it draped her like a funereal shroud, and all that remained were the grunts of the thing on top of her, the pain between her legs, and the feel of warm blood as it trickled from her throat to her chest.

* * * *

In her apartment and stretched out across her bed, as if all is right with the world, Carla awakens from the most restful sleep she's ever had. It takes her a moment or two to realize she's no longer in that awful cell, but once she does, she sits up and rubs her eyes, bringing her bare feet around to the cold floor.

"My baby…"

She springs to her feet, feeling stronger than before, and searches the small apartment. Her son is not there.

Carla dresses quickly, pulling on a pair of old comfortable jeans and a heavy sweater. She's just finishing pushing her feet into a pair of boots when there is a quiet knock on the door. Quickly searching for something to defend herself with, a weapon—anything—she settles on a small steak knife she finds in one of the kitchen drawers.

After tucking the knife into the back of her jeans and covering it with the sweater, she answers the door.

Suzie stands there smiling at her, Carla's son in her arms. "There you are," she says, beaming. "How you feeling, kiddo? You look great. Doesn't Mommy look great?"

Forcing a smile, Carla reaches out and takes the child from her. "Thanks," she says, kissing her son's cheek then hugging him tight.

Suzie walks in, closes the door behind her, then glances around as if expecting something or someone else. "You just wake up?"

You know I did, Carla thinks. *I don't know how, but you do.*

"Yeah," she says. "I don't think I've ever slept so soundly."

"It's good, right?" Suzie winks and wanders over toward the kitchen table. "Didn't I tell you things would get better?"

"You did."

"Few more days and you'll be perfect. Just like us." Suzie gives her a conspiratorial smile. "Forever, kiddo…*forever*…"

Carla nods, returning her knowing smile.

"Anyway, Lou wanted me to tell you he'll be back in a couple hours. He wants to discuss things with you now that you're, well, you know, more *aware*."

You're not going to help me, Carla thinks. *You never were.*

"Okay," she says, forcing another smile. "Was the baby okay?"

"He's been just fine, a real doll. He's Lou's pride and joy, that one. You'd think it was the only kid he ever fathered or something."

"Have there been a lot?"

"More than he remembers, probably," Suzie says. "But you got to keep populating the nests, right?"

Carla nods.

"The baby did miss his afternoon nap, though, so you can probably put him down right now if you want to."

Carla excuses herself and takes him to the crib. She sits him down amidst a couple stuffed animals and he snuggles in quickly and drifts off to sleep.

She gently rubs his little back. He's the warmest thing in this awful cold place.

I may be one of them, but my son will never be part of this. Never.

When she rejoins Suzie in the kitchen, Carla looks to the window. Night has fallen. There's not much time, and if she's to attempt what she has never had the courage and strength to try before, she has to hurry.

"Well," Carla says, "thanks for bringing him back."

"No problem." Suzie shrugs. "Lou said to hang around, keep you company until he gets here. Want to play cards or—"

"Sure, sit down." Carla motions to the table, her heart and mind racing, and yet, she feels a strange control, a cool steadiness. "I'll get the deck."

Suzie plops down onto one of the kitchen chairs, her back to Carla. "Put some coffee on too, would you?"

"Be happy to."

Carla moves to the counter, opens the drawer where the cards are, then tosses them over Suzie's shoulder onto the table. They hit and spread out, some sliding to the floor.

"Jesus," Suzie says irritably, "what the hell's that about, girl?"

Carla stands behind her, waiting for her to retrieve a card from the floor. Once she has, Carla pulls free the knife, grabs a handful of Suzie's hair, yanks her head back, and stabs the knife into the center of her throat.

Eyes wide with shock, arms flailing and legs kicking, Suzie cries out.

She tries to fight but her better days are well behind her. Carla is the strong one now, her superior.

Her cries quickly turn to disturbing gurgling sounds as Carla rips the serrated blade across Suzie's throat, pushing it as deep as she can as she saws back and forth.

Despite her newfound strength, it still takes three attempts, but once Suzie's throat is slit clean across, she's already lost so much blood she's barely conscious.

Carla steps back, her hands covered in blood, her face flecked with it from the initial spray. Suzie looks at her, still shocked, the blood pumping from her throat to form enormous puddles across the table and floor. Those eyes roll to white, her body slumps to the side, and she falls from the chair, collapsing into a bloody heap on the kitchen floor.

The blood does nothing for Carla. If anything, the violence should repulse her. But it doesn't. She feels nothing. Before, she was so timid and frightened all the time. Now she feels powerful, capable…cruel…and yet, she still has enough of her true self to know that if her child has any chance at a better life away from all this, she must do it now. Or she never will.

She steps away from the growing puddle of crimson. This is not the blood she craves. It's identical to that which flows through her veins, and therefore not wholly human. And it is human blood on which she now feeds.

Carla drops the knife, goes to the sink and washes the blood from her hands and face as best she can. When she's finished, she hurries back to the crib, grabs her son, and wraps him in a blanket from head to toe. Thankfully he is still asleep, but she holds him close so if he should come awake he won't see the carnage.

She goes to the window, looks down into the street. There's a ledge, a fire escape to its left. How many times has she fantasized about climbing down those stairs, stepping onto the walk, and running as far away as she can? The fear has always prevented her. But she is no longer afraid. She is strong.

Do it. Do it now.

Carla lifts the window with her free hand, feels cold winter air hit her face. Voices sound from the entrance below. Are Lou's men guarding the doors? Her heart flutters with anticipation.

I'll slaughter anyone that tries to stop me.

She listens a moment. Even her hearing is stronger, more focused and precise. The voices down below gradually fade, leaving behind occasional bursts of winter wind. The building is quiet, dark.

Just beyond the window, the ledge is littered with patches of ice and some snow. Beneath the glow of the moon, more ice shines ominously along the fire escape.

Carla opens the window as far as it will go then gingerly sits on the sill. She swings her right leg out first, then her left, and steps down onto the ledge.

The night air gets even colder, and the smell of the nearby sea fills her nostrils. There's also a burning smell somewhere in the distance, the sickening and sweet smell of human flesh.

She presses her back flat against the building, swaying a bit as a flurry of wind hits. The fire escape isn't that far, maybe twenty feet.

You can make it.

Slowly, Carla slides sideways, free hand moving over brick, her body so cold, she begins to shiver. She suddenly slips a bit on the ice but catches her balance with agility she has never before possessed. Controlling her breathing, she remains still for a minute or so, and then begins again.

Sirens sound in the distance, and a man's voice calls out, echoing from somewhere deep in the cold night.

Is someone watching her?

Be careful, there are bad things out here in the night.

The fire escape is closer now, just a short climb to the bottom—to the street—to freedom.

Carla's descent is easier than she anticipated, but remaining cautious, she carefully though deliberately makes her way to the walk beneath the building. She sighs with relief when she realizes no one is standing guard at the door, and a quick glimpse reveals an empty lobby as well.

More lies from Lou.

She looks up at the dark, shaded windows.

Then she runs, holding her baby close. Another dark phantom absorbed into the dreamscape of a freezing winter night.

CHAPTER 22

IT IS THE LARGE GRANITE STEPS, and those she finds standing atop them, that bring her to a stop. Out of breath and freezing, with the baby still half asleep but crying gently in her arms, Carla stands before an old church.

The nuns watch her from their perch, shrouded in black habits slightly darker than the night. One breaks from the others and slowly moves forward, slowly descending the steps. As she gets closer, Carla realizes she is a young woman, perhaps a few years younger than herself.

As Carla recognizes God in her eyes, the nun recognizes something far more sinister in hers. She stops, hesitates a few steps from where Carla stands.

Before, Carla would've sought sanctuary. She knows that's no longer possible for her. But it is for her son.

"My baby," Carla gasps. "Please take him. Protect him."

The nun cocks her head, trying for a better look at the child.

Carla holds him up, pulls back enough of the blanket to reveal the child's face, his little cheeks bright red in the cold. "Please," she says.

"Who are you?" the nun asks in a quiet voice.

"No one," she says. "Nothing..."

"Not in the eyes of God."

Carla trembles, fighting her new natural desire to recoil from this place and the nun standing before her. "It's too late for me," she says. "But he can still be saved. Please help him. I don't have much time."

Slowly, the nun nods her head.

As the realization hits her, Carla begins to weep. She cuddles her son close, peppering him with so many kisses he comes awake and begins to cry. "I love you, I love you, I love you," she whispers through her tears.

Sobbing, she delivers her child to the nun's waiting arms. He fusses at first, squirms around a bit, but then settles and quiets, resting his head against her arms.

"What is his name?" the nun asks.

"Joseph," Carla says, slowly backing away. "My son's name is *Joseph*."

* * * *

Fog rolls in off the roiling ocean, covering the city in an eerie mist.

Carla walks slowly through the empty streets, the cold wind slicing right through her. She moves differently now, like a hunter. Her whole life, Carla has been preyed upon and used. No more. Now she is the hunter.

She will no longer fear, but *be* feared.

Her transition is nearly complete.

Yet even in this horrible moment, when she realizes she will never again see her child, she knows she will not hunt alone. It is not the nature of who she is now, who she has become. What she has become.

We hunt in packs.

At the corner, less than two blocks from the building, Lou steps into view beneath a beam of a streetlight. The fog wraps around him, slinking through the light. He watches her, a huge knife in his hand.

Others wait nearby in the shadows. The others in their nest...*her* nest...

"The boy," Lou growls.

Carla shakes her head no, and somehow, as their eyes meet, words pass between them. Words she and he can hear in their minds, laced with the growls and snarls of an ancient brethren that exist in them both now.

We are one.

"You had no right," Lou tells her.

"And you have no power where he is now. None of our kind does."

"Wanna bet? I should kill you. I should rip you to fucking shreds."

"We both know you won't." Carla stands defiant.

"You have to answer for Suzie."

"She was old and stupid. We're stronger without her."

Lou watches her a while, weighing the validity of her statement. "Come home then," he says, lowering the knife. "The home I've made for you."

Is this still a dream, she wonders. *Or am I dead?*

"Yes," Lou says, answering her thoughts.

The others step out of the dark. She waits as they form a half circle around her, and then together, they slowly walk toward Lou.

Lou takes her hand. His flesh is always so cold, but now so is hers.

He smiles. It is the Devil's smile, so Carla chooses, one last time, to remember instead the smile of the only man she ever truly loved.

Chris, I remember it all.

And finally, she remembers Joseph's face too, those big dark eyes gazing up at her as she held him tight.

She knows that just like the bits and pieces of her that still remain, these memories will soon be gone as well, stolen by the darkness like everything else. So for now, she savors them.

You're free, Joseph. I pray the horror is over for you.

But for Carla, it is just beginning.

The dark shapes surrounding her float closer, wrapping their arms around her, pulling her closer into their fold, their nest.

And somewhere in the darkest recesses of her mind, Carla hears the cracking bones of a man screaming in agony and begging for mercy that will never come.

She takes Lou's arm as they walk away. The infernos of Hell nip at their heels as they head for the darkest of places, one of mist and the freshly turned dirt of musty graves, nightmares and orgies of unimaginable sex, blood and violence.

Not quite Perdition, but one of the last stops along the way.

Together, they drift into darkness. The night swallows its children whole.

In their wake, all that remains is fog gently rolling along an empty street.

As if they were never really there at all.

PART THREE

GATE OF DREAMS

"Not a great while ago, passing through the gate of dreams, I visited that region of the earth in which lies the famous City of Destruction."
—Nathaniel Hawthorne

CHAPTER 23

HIS DREAMS HAVE BEEN CHANGING. They're different than before, dark and disturbing, confusing. He dreams of burning, rolling around in the snow on fire, set ablaze and trying desperately to get the flames off of him. Others stand nearby, watching with eyes long dead. They do nothing to help him, because they are not upset. They are pleased. The fire is not killing him, but changing him, transforming him into someone else. Some*thing* else...

When he dreams now, he dreams of the night, of tombs lined with old coffins draped in spider webs, of dirt and rot and the stink from ancient graves. And pain. A kind of agony that leaves him riddled with savage, sinister, primeval fury. Until he awakens, and it all slides away into the fog of what feels like faded memories. But he knows that can't be what they are. He tells himself they're just nightmares, and does his best to leave them where they belong, scattered across the bizarre dreamscapes that inhabit one's subconscious mind.

But these have been his dreams.

Until now...

Your soul is no longer your own.

With those cryptic words in his ears and the lingering stench of something burning filling his nostrils, fire ignites and a flame rises. The world goes blind as the fire burns, mingling with the crisp morning air and wafting about like a mass of spirits lost in the distorted chaos of space and time.

From the stairs that lead to the tunnels beneath the city, the tortured shrieks of the damned drift up and onto the street, as if calling for mercy.

Marco brings the lighter to the tip of his cigarette and draws until it burns hot. As he inhales the smoke deep into his lungs, the screams become the screech of a braking subway car below ground.

Ignoring the chill along the length of his spine, Marco exhales, shuffles his feet against the cold, wipes his nose, then considers his surroundings.

He finds himself on a street corner, but cannot remember how he came to be here. *Weird*, he thinks. This kind of thing has never happened to him before. He's always together, in control, and knows the score. He parties, sometimes harder than he probably should, but he can handle it. He's always handled it.

This, however, is not that. This is something *different*.

Of average height, with a trim, well-muscled physique and dark brown hair he slicks straight back from his handsome face, Marco Finzione is clad in a brown leather jacket, a tight pullover jersey, black jeans, and low-heeled black boots. An earring in the shape of a cross dangles from his left ear, a thick gold herringbone bracelet adorns his right wrist, and he wears a pinky ring with a small but beautiful diamond on his left hand. Though only in his early twenties, as always, Marco is neat and clean and impeccably groomed, not a hair out of place. He carries himself like the young lion he is, not with arrogance, but an effortless charm and confidence, as if he is somehow unaware of these gifts and has been granted them without his knowledge.

Marco does understand how fortunate he is in other areas, however. His is a working-class family that has always provided him with a nice home and all the necessities of life. More importantly, his parents are both kind and loving and completely devoted to him, their only child. He was raised in a safe and deeply nurturing environment, with never any shortage of love and affection and encouragement. As a result, he treasures his mother and father and the home and upbringing they provided him. Even now that he's been on his own for a couple years, he still visits them regularly and spends as much time with them as possible.

Although thinking of his parents calms and reassures him, it does nothing to solve the mystery of how he has come to be here, so he smokes his cigarette and looks around. Marco knows this neighborhood. It's only a few short blocks from his apartment building. He's stood on this corner and walked along this street countless times. But that's not the point, because he still has no memory of how he came to be here on such a brutally cold morning.

He checks his watch then crosses the street, weaving his way through the light traffic until he reaches the opposite corner. This is where he catches the bus to work each day. Again, nothing unusual, and yet…

The bus arrives before he finishes his cigarette. He flicks it into the street then boards, the only new passenger at his stop this morning.

When he climbs the steps, he realizes he's also the only passenger on the bus. All the seats are empty.

Usually the driver is a friendly Jamaican woman named Lois who always talks him up and jokes with him. Today it's an older and irritable looking man he's never seen before.

Marco pays his fare, hesitating as he considers the empty bus before him.

"Take your seat," the driver says.

"This is a first." Marco flashes a beautiful smile. "Nobody else here, huh?"

The driver audibly sighs, looks over his shoulder with what seems to be an inordinate amount of effort, and then with a dramatic grunt, turns back to Marco. "Do you *see* anybody else onboard, hotshot?"

"Just making conversation," Marco tells him.

As he strolls down the aisle, he hears the driver behind him mumble, "Kid, you want conversation, join a lonely hearts club."

The door closes and the bus lurches forward.

Marco drops into a seat at about the halfway point of the bus and slides over to the window. He takes out his phone, opens one of his game apps and settles in, as his is about a ten minute ride to the very edge of the city, that small area just shy of the suburbs, where he works.

Usually the bus makes several stops, and by the time he reaches his destination it's packed with passengers. Today, the driver makes no further stops, and Marco rides alone.

When he disembarks and steps down into the mall parking lot, he looks back at the driver and gives a quick wave. "Thanks," he says. "See you around."

The driver shakes his head, as if to say, *you poor clueless bastard*, and then closes the door and drives off.

With a shrug, Marco heads for the mall entrance. Once inside, he waits a moment for his eyes to adjust from the bright outdoors to the artificial mall light.

What lies before him rivals the most demonic of possessions.

A gradually dying monument to disposable income, the mall has become an abandoned ghost town. Empty kiosks, dead escalators, barren store windows, and barred doorways; it's all a showcase for the forgotten now, as vacant as the faceless souls that once used this place to satisfy their gluttonous lust for greed and consumption.

The only remnants—at least at this early hour—are the aged drifters, the seniors walking up and down, back and forth along the otherwise deserted fairway, shuffling about like zombies, or perhaps ghosts of the earlier eras from which they come. Beneath the dull, synthetic light, they barely appear human. But then, under such circumstances, who could?

Ironic, Marco thinks, finding himself among these material-world spirits, since he's fairly certain everyone thinks him some sort of superhuman. Marco has never considered himself anything special, but others do. He's smart and handsome and funny and kind. At least that's what people tell him. Guys his own age look up to him and often tell him they wish they *were* him, while women of all ages adore him. Even a lot of men are attracted to him that way. Everyone thinks he's on a fast track to success, despite the fact that he's just a lowly shoe salesman at a store in the local mall who, once the rent is paid and the groceries bought, spends all his money on clothes and jewelry and cigarettes.

His girlfriend Ginger thinks he's *blessed.* That's the word she always uses, she of the skin so smooth it might've been made from wax, the ice-blue eyes, small nose, playfully frowny mouth, the body forged in Hell, and the hair for days that hangs just below her shoulders in big blonde waves. She's always reminded Marco of a living doll, sentient and physically animated, but somehow just short of actual. Just the same, she's the kind of girl that's so beautiful men literally stop and stare, mouths open, not even attempting to mask their lust. Some women are certain men's types. Ginger is every man's type. In fact, she's most human beings' type. Everyone is attracted to Ginger. It's as if people are defenseless against her, which in a way, Marco supposes, they are. The problem is when she reveals what lies beyond the beauty, because for many, while she's gorgeous and undeniably sweet, *her* blessings more or less end there. She is, as some might cruelly say, not the sharpest tool in the shed. Still, Marco knows he should be happier that she's with him, or was, but somehow their relationship, while fun, has never been something he's taken all that seriously.

And that, according to Ginger, is his biggest shortcoming.

"You have all this potential and so many blessings, so many advantages a lot of people never have," she has said to him many times. "Everyone sees it but you. All you do is go through the motions and work that stupid job at the mall when you could do so much more. You just don't take things seriously."

Marco has repeatedly assured her that he does, in fact, take many *things* seriously. He just doesn't take himself seriously. Why the hell should he? He'll have his whole life to be serious. He's a young man, free and fun and exploring, still finding his way through life to whomever and whatever he'll one day become. He's still a work in progress, he always tells her, but evidently that isn't enough. She feels that if he would only make the right moves they could become a power couple, whatever that is, and that his lack of effort is holding them both back.

Two weeks ago, Ginger broke up with him and fled to the other side of the country to stay with family awhile. She's gone about as far as one can go, to the desert. With barely a goodbye she packed her bags and off she went, and Marco has not heard from or spoken to her since.

For a time, he seriously considered following her, as inexplicably he feels drawn to desert regions himself. He's thought about deserts for as long as he can remember—the sand and sun and dryness, the stone and scorched earth, the vastness of it all—though he has no idea why. It strikes him as fate, though he's willing to also entertain the possibility that it may simply be obsession.

He can't be sure.

Marco decides to contemplate such things over breakfast, so he heads for the food court, where at least two or three places are still in business and open before anyone else.

As he moves between the walking dead, he remembers the strange detached voice and those bizarre words in his mind.

Your soul is not your own.

It frightens him, though he can't pinpoint why. Maybe he should chalk it up to those disturbing nightmares he's been having lately.

He continues to contemplate these things until a few minutes later, when he sits on a bench across from the shoe store where he works and instead digs into a breakfast burrito. One of only six retail establishments still operational in the entire mall, despite a decided lack of business for some time now, the shoe store has somehow remained open.

As Marco eats his breakfast, he's interrupted by an elderly homeless woman he knows only by the odd street name of Peanut Pie. She has begun to preach while walking the mall, as she is known to do. The craziest of the fairway drifters, she stumbles about with a ratty old Bible in hand, and today, announces at the top of her lungs that she will begin with Psalm 28:4.

"Give them according to their deeds, and according to the wickedness of their endeavors: give them after the work of their hands; render to them their desert!"

That final word hits Marco's gut with even more weight than the burrito.

He knows this cannot be coincidence. He is meant to hear this for some reason. Although he's Catholic, he hasn't gone to church since he was in high school, and he's anything but a biblical scholar. But it does seem to mean those who are evil flee to deserts, or at a minimum, wind up there. Of course, Marco refuses to believe everyone who lives in or around a desert is evil, as that's preposterous, but he suspects it's addressing those who feel *drawn* to such places due to their sins. Perhaps one eventually heeds this calling, or simply succumbs to it for reasons they don't fully understand. Could this be why he feels compelled to seek out the dry lands? Could this be a message from the spirit world meant just for him, delivered through the vessel of a seemingly deranged homeless woman? Or is he putting too much stock in things he's never taken seriously, much less literally?

Even Jesus went to the desert and found his destiny there, he thinks.

He also found the Devil.

This makes Marco fear what *he* might find. What if the desert is not as pleased to see him as he is it? What if it has plans for him far more sinister in nature than healing?

It could also be he just misses Ginger. It really could be that simple. Or it could just as easily be something else, something beyond his comprehension.

Something horrific and evil, he thinks, though he has no idea why such dark and dramatic thoughts occur to him just then.

These are indeed strange days.

Peanut Pie shuffles away, waving her Bible around and shouting out more verses, none of which have anything to do with the desert.

Marco is still not sure what to make of this. The only thing he is sure of is that he doesn't miss Ginger nearly as much as he feared he might. This makes him sad, and more than a little guilty, as he knows he should. But sitting here thinking about things and quietly munching his breakfast, he admits part of him is actually glad she's gone.

She'll be happier, he tells himself.

He doesn't know if that's true, but it makes him feel better to believe it, because he wishes nothing but good things for her. Ginger deserves happiness with a man that can give her what she needs, and far as Marco can determine, he is not that man. He has no desire to be.

Right around the time he finishes the burrito, Marco sees his boss Edgar approaching. Clad in one of his typical outfits of polyester stretch slacks, gum-soled shoes, an old parka over a short sleeved shirt and a cheap tie (a clip-on), in one hand he carries a cardboard tray holding a large Styrofoam cup of coffee and a breakfast sandwich, and in the other a set of keys to the grate currently pulled down and secured over the entrance to the store.

Forty-nine years old, with a wife and three kids at home, including a daughter that is severely disabled, Edgar has worked in the retail field since high school, and for this particular shoe store chain for the last twenty-one years. Slovenly and overweight, Edgar wears his badly thinning hair in a comb-over that is both hideous and a marvel of modern engineering. A mall creature, he seldom sees the outdoors, fresh air, or sunshine. For decades now he's worked in this artificial environment—twelve hours a day, six days a week—beneath the dull glow of artificial light, breathing predominantly recycled artificial air. And it shows. His skin is pasty, his eyes are saddled with dark bags, and he complains frequently of headaches. Edgar has a perpetually weary look to him, like he hasn't slept in days and if he doesn't sit down soon his legs are going to give out. Sadly, he's dying as surely as this once booming palace is, and just as gradually, a little more each day.

Although Edgar has always been good to him, and Marco is very fond of him, he also sees his boss as a reminder of what he doesn't want to be or ever become. Marco's only been working at the mall a short time, and the way things are headed, the mall won't be in existence much longer anyway, which is fine because he has come to the determination that a life in retail is not for him. For now, it's a living, but for Marco, it's only a stop along the way to what he is sure will be a better and more fulfilling life.

When he's close enough to unlock the security grate, Edgar greets Marco with the same phrase he always uses. "What do you say, what do you know?"

Marco stands, tosses his burrito wrapper in a nearby bin, and joins his boss at the front of the store. "Hey, Edgar," he says.

"Sorry I'm a little late, champ. Colder than Eskimo pussy out there, my goddamn car took forever to start. Think I need a new battery. Hell, I need a whole new car." With his free hand, he raises the gate. "Come on, I got to talk to you about some stuff first thing."

Once the grate retracts, they enter the store. Marco waits by the sales desk while Edgar goes into the stockroom out back and turns on the lights.

Marco watches as all around him the store comes to life. He leans against the desk and waits until Edgar returns from the back, sans jacket, and joins him.

"What's up?" Marco asks. "Did I screw up the paperwork or something?"

Rather than answer, Edgar fumbles his coffee from the tray, sets it on the desk, then holds an envelope out for Marco.

"What's this?"

"Your paycheck," Edgar tells him.

"But today's not payday." He tears the envelope open, looks at the amount on the check. "And this is way more than I make."

"It's this and next week's pay." Edgar won't look at him, focusing instead on adding numerous sugars and a few creamers to his enormous coffee. "I got to let you go, champ. I'm sorry, it came from corporate, there's nothing I can do. You know if there was anything I could do I'd do it, right?"

Though disappointed, Marco isn't surprised. "Yeah," he says, "of course."

"They're closing the store next week," Edgar explains.

"No way," he says, though again, he's not surprised. "What are you going to do?"

"I'm being transferred to another location. I don't know which one yet, supposed to hear something today. Probably have to settle for an assistant manager position until another opening comes up, if it does. I tried to save your job, but, well, you know how it is with corporate."

"I know." Marco smiles, slaps him on the shoulder. "It's cool."

"At least I got you an extra week's pay out of the cheap bastards."

"Thanks, man." Marco slips the envelope into his pocket. "I'll be okay."

"You're right, you'll be fine." Edgar tears into his breakfast sandwich with the grace of a hyena devouring a recent kill. "You're an absolute all-star," he says, chewing noisily with his mouth open. "Why waste your life in this shit bin? Go get yourself some high-powered sales gig. You'll make more money than you know what to do with. You're a natural salesman. I've always told you that. Haven't I always told you that? You're smart, good-looking, and a damn fine talker. Too honest, but you'll get over that. Just do me a solid, champ. Make sure you remember your old bud Edgar when you're decked out in silk suits, driving a Porsche and neck deep in classy pussy, okay?"

"Okay, Edgar," Marco says with a chuckle.

"So you, ah…" Edgar tears off another bite. "You stay in touch."

"You too," Marco says. "I'll give you a call sometime. We'll go get some drinks, maybe catch a game on TV."

Edgar nods and looks away. "Yeah, sure," he says, though he knows this will probably never happen. "Take care of yourself, champ."

Five minutes later Marco is back at the food court. It's a bit busier now, but not much. He sits at one of the empty tables and thinks about how he'll spend the rest of his day. Although he's sad about losing his job, on the other hand he feels a wonderful sense of freedom and opportunity as well.

He purchases a small local newspaper from a nearby kiosk, then returns to his table and opens it to the HELP WANTED section. Unfortunately, there's not much in the way of good jobs. At least not the ones he's qualified for. The sales positions are all either car or insurance gigs he has no interest in. He checks a few sites on his phone with the same results. Marco's not entirely sure what he should do now. The shoe store is the only real job he's ever had. He's never been let go before. With a sigh, he pushes the paper away and decides to go back outside and have a cigarette, maybe catch the bus back home and—

"Marco, how *are* you?"

A man he knows only as Billy is suddenly standing before him. At one time he worked as a tailor at a high-end clothing store in the mall, but it closed several months ago and Marco hasn't seen him since. He doesn't know the man well, but they used to chat now and then when Billy still worked at the mall, as the older man quickly took a shine to him from the first time they met, standing at the counter of an Orange Julius in the center of the mall enjoying a hot dog lunch. Perhaps three or four times since, he has visited Marco at the shoe store, and once even bought a pair of calfskin loafers from him, but their conversations, while jovial, have always been superficial at best. Edgar always teased Marco about the older man's attention, and routinely referred to him as "*that creepy old fruit*," but Marco finds his jokes offensive and thinks of Billy as a harmless older man, an eccentric and lonely sort who probably doesn't have many friends.

The dude's a major perv, a real weirdo, Edgar always says. *Everybody knows he is, champ, it's not even a secret. Ask around, you'll see.*

But Marco has never *asked around*, and sees no reason to. He takes people one at a time, and doesn't pay much attention to what others say. Billy has never been anything but nice to him, and sure, maybe he flirts a little—if that's even what it is—but so what?

"Hey, Billy," he says. The man is always meticulously groomed and nicely dressed, but he must be in his late sixties or early seventies by now, and Marco has never felt comfortable referring to a man old enough to be his grandfather by his first name. Billy, however, has always insisted, and has never revealed his last name anyway. "I haven't seen you in a while. Working at the mall again?"

"Oh, good Lord no!" Billy self-consciously runs his perfectly manicured fingers through his neatly combed silver hair. "I've finally retired. At least from tailoring, that is. These days I spend most of my time on photography, and *that* I have been *thoroughly* enjoying. How's everything at the shoe store?"

"Actually, believe it or not, I just got fired."

"No!" Billy places a hand flat against his chest, mussing his beautifully pressed shirt. "How *could* they? You're such a marvelous salesman!"

"They're closing the store next week."

He frowns and straightens his blue blazer even though it doesn't require straightening. "And the company had nothing else for you?"

"Didn't even offer," Marco says with a shrug.

"Well it's their loss, the bastards. Let's hope it's a blessing in disguise."

"I guess I'll find out."

"I'm sorry you've had a bad time this morning," Billy says, offering a wide smile of perfectly capped square white teeth. "But it's *so* nice to see you again."

"Good to see you too, Billy."

His dark eyes—sometimes so dark they appear almost black—search Marco's. "Tell me, do you have any *immediate* plans?"

"You mean right this minute?"

"Right this very minute," he says with a quick wink.

"Not really, no."

"Splendid!" Billy steps closer, leaning in with a conspiratorial grin. "As it turns out, my schedule is wide open. I realize it's early, but I've never been much for *restraint*, as it were, so why don't you let me buy you lunch and a drink or two and we'll celebrate our newfound freedom together? It's so much more fun than doing it alone, and maybe if we're lucky we'll be able to make today a little more tolerable, hmm?"

Fuck it, Marco thinks, *why not? I got nothing else to do, maybe I should.*

What he doesn't realize yet is that the manner in which he answers this question will either save him or forever change the trajectory of his life.

Because his soul is not his own.

CHAPTER 24

AS THE TAXI PULLS UP IN front of an old three-story building, Marco looks out his window and squints. He and Billy have spent the day at a nearby watering hole, and have had so many drinks Marco lost count hours ago.

Billy's drunken laughter distracts him a moment. He's giggling over some quip he made that Marco didn't quite hear, but he laughs politely anyway.

After paying the driver, they both tumble out of the cab and stagger toward the building. Billy bursts into laughter again, over what Marco isn't quite sure, but he's certain that at this point it no longer matters anyway.

It's near dark, and even colder than it was previously. A light snow blows about, not accumulating, at least not yet, but it stops Marco in his tracks. He stares at the whirlwind of flakes surrounding them, certain it is the most beautiful thing he has ever seen.

Billy stops short alongside him and looks too. "I love the snow," he says.

"I like the heat better, but sometimes snow is so beautiful you can't help but love it." Marco tilts back his head and lets the flakes hit his face. "It reminds me I'm alive on planet Earth."

Billy grabs his arm, falls into him drunkenly. "What a profoundly lovely thing to say. I always suspected you had the heart of a young poet."

"It's at my apartment," Marco says, beaming. "I keep it in the fridge. Maybe I'll show it to you sometime."

They stare at each other a moment, neither terribly steady on their feet. And then Billy lets out another burst of laughter and slaps Marco on the back. "I love your dark sense of humor," he says fondly. "But I am also *fah-reezing*." Billy releases his arm and makes a formal, dramatic, bent-at-the-waist sweeping gesture toward the double front doors of the building. "So please, do a cold and shivering old man a favor and accept this invitation to my humble abode!"

Marco looks at the building. Though still very drunk, the icy air helps to focus him somewhat. His eyes scan the double doors, the glass center panel, and the beautiful little butterflies etched into it. Something from deep within him rises and bubbles into the base of his throat like heartburn. "This building," he says, stomach grumbling and making him wish he hadn't eaten so many greasy appetizers at the bar. "I swear I've seen it before."

"You've likely been by it, no? It's quite old, one of the oldest in the city, in fact. There are several apartments in addition to mine, maybe you've been here before or know one of the other residents?"

Marco doesn't recall ever being to or even coming across this building prior. He lives on the other side of town in what is a much nicer neighborhood, and until this moment never knew where Billy lived, so that can't explain it either. Yet there remains something eerily and unquestionably familiar about this place.

Something across the street catches Marco's attention. Near the mouth of a nearby alley, a fire burns in a metal barrel. A group of homeless people are gathered around it, warming themselves as best they can.

Sad, he thinks, and then winces as a sharp pain fires through his temple.

"Are you all right?" Billy asks, arching a silver eyebrow.

The pain is gone as quickly as it arrived. Marco returns his focus to the building. "It's just…I feel like I've been here before, but I know I haven't."

From Billy's expression he can tell he must not be making sense. Multiple shots of Jameson and numerous Long Island Iced Teas will do that to a person.

"Never mind," Marco says softly. "Too much to drink, I guess."

"I am wholly unfamiliar with this *too much* concept you speak of, so I suggest we go inside, warm up, and immediately begin depleting my personal stash of alcoholic beverages as quickly and efficiently as possible." Billy's face suddenly turns serious. "Although I do believe one should only accept invitations one truly wishes to receive."

"That makes sense. I think." Marco laughs. "Let's get out of this cold."

Billy takes him by the arm and leads him to the entrance. As they slip into a foyer with a black-and-white checkerboard tile floor, Billy closes and secures the door behind them.

"Don't get me wrong, a little caution is never a bad idea. Particularly in the absence of light, one should always take great care." The old man scrutinizes the growing darkness from which they've come, a smile that looks suspiciously like a snarl curling his lips. "After all, there are bad things out there in the night."

* * * *

The building is quiet, and even once they've made the climb to the third floor, they fail to come across anyone else. Once they finally enter Billy's apartment, Marco is surprised to discover how small it is. He expects something more lavish, given the way the man carries himself and dresses. And after all those years of work, is this all he can afford? Marco feels bad for him. Maybe something happened that forced him to live in such a place at his advanced age.

A single room with a dated kitchen, there is a neatly made, inexpensive looking bed that looks like something out of a prison, a small loveseat with a bright red floral pattern that seems out of place in such an otherwise drab apartment, and against the main wall, a large film screen hangs, a small table in front of it that houses what appears to be some sort of projector. Along the other wall is an old cast iron radiator, and a couple metal filing cabinets directly across from it, an old camcorder sitting atop one. There is no bathroom. Billy explains there's one located at the end of the hall.

"And you thought I was joking when I said *humble* abode!" He smiles, though self-consciously. "I know it's not much, and the neighborhood isn't exactly *posh*, but it suits my modest needs and has allowed me to save quite a bit of money over the years."

"It's nice," Marco lies. "Hell, my place isn't any bigger."

"I don't plan to live in the city forever." Billy moves to the kitchen, pulls several bottles of liquor from one of the cabinets and places them, along with two glasses, on the counter. "I've saved enough to go anywhere in the world I'd like. I just have to choose a destination and finally convince...*myself*...to do it."

Marco drifts into the kitchen. There is a metal table with two chairs, so he steadies himself against that and watches while Billy pours them both a drink. "Where are you thinking of going?" he asks.

"Somewhere warm," Billy says, filling a small ice bucket with cubes from the freezer. "Much as I love snow, I've grown tired of the cold."

Marco thinks about Ginger in some desert town, and wonders if Billy has ever thought about the desert too. "Sometimes I like it, but most of the time I'd rather be somewhere warmer too."

"Maybe you can come along." Billy winks then hands him a drink before taking one for himself. "Wouldn't that be fun?"

After a short obligatory laugh, Marco takes the drink and looks back at the other part of the room. "Is that a movie projector?" he asks.

"It is." Billy stands next to him and motions to the screen with his drink. "I don't have much use for television, don't even have one, and as I mentioned to you earlier, I've been doing a lot of photography and filming. I find this is the best way to view my work."

"Cool, you make your own movies?"

"Yes, in a way."

Marco takes a sip of his drink, which reminds him how drunk he already is. "That's awesome, Billy. What kind of things do you make?"

"We can take a look later if you'd like." Billy strolls over to the loveseat. "They're nothing special. Mostly *experimental*, I suppose you could say. They're quite useful not only artistically, but in other ways as well."

Marco doesn't know what he means but nods like he does.

"Please, have a seat."

Marco thinks a moment. Other than the kitchen table, the only places to sit are on Billy's bed or joining him on the loveseat. He reaches for one of the chairs so he can turn it and face Billy before sitting down.

"You don't have to stay way over there. Come." Billy pats the vacant part of the loveseat. "Sit next to me. I don't hear as well as I used to and I don't have to tell you I'm three sheets to the wind at the moment, so indulge an old man."

He really doesn't want to sit that close, but what the hell. Marco feels sorry for the guy. "Sure," he says, and within a few steps, he's reached the small couch. "No problem. And thanks for the drink."

"Don't be silly, it's my pleasure," Billy says, beaming as Marco sits down. "Have as much as you'd like. I know I plan to!"

"Cool."

"Cool indeed." Billy's smile drifts away, and he looks down into his drink before taking a big sip. "I don't know why you've always been so kind to me, Marco, but I want you to know I really do appreciate your friendship."

"Hey, it's no big deal." Marco sips his drink. "You're a good guy."

"Well thank you, but I know how a lot of people at the mall talked about me behind my back." His face grows dark. "Always making fun of me or accusing me of things. I know all about it. I heard their slurs and snickers, saw the disapproving scowls and sideways glances. Everything from how I'm some lecherous queer to a pervert that sexually accosts women when given the chance. Apparently I'm an equal opportunity offender."

"I don't listen to what people say," Marco tells him.

"Be that as it may, I'm sure you've heard plenty about me." He runs his fingers through his silver hair. "And most of it is probably true."

Marco laughs.

This time Billy sports a playful expression but doesn't join him.

"I make my own decisions," Marco explains. "Even about people—hell—especially about people."

Billy's eyes lift from his drink, lock onto Marco's. "That's very wise."

"I don't know, seems like common sense to me."

A subtle smile purses Billy's lips. "You really are quite a remarkable young man, aren't you?"

"I'm just me, Billy."

"Well, here's to you." He raises his glass.

Marco taps his glass against Billy's. "And you."

"To us then! Even better!"

"To us!"

They laugh and drink some more and then grow quiet. As Billy staggers back into the kitchen to get them each another drink, Marco glances at the only window in the apartment. Night has fallen and the snow looks to have gotten a bit heavier. He knows he should probably start thinking about calling for an Uber or getting a taxi and heading home before the snow gets too heavy, but he's comfortable and drunk and warm, so he decides to stick around for one or two more drinks.

"Looks like quite a storm developing out there," Billy says, as if he's read Marco's mind. He returns with the drinks, hands one to his guest, then sits down next to him. "Don't worry, you can stay the night if need be."

"Thanks, but I'll probably take off in a little while."

"Just take good care, lots of crazies out there these days."

"Always lots of crazies in the city," Marco says. "It's nothing new."

"That's true, of course, but of late, one band of crazies out there is *particularly* heinous."

Marco thinks about what he said. "You mean the homeless people that've been getting set on fire? That's a group of people doing it? I figured it was just some psycho, probably one of their own."

"I hear it's more than just the homeless." Billy raises his eyebrows with conspiratorial glee. "They say there's a coven hidden somewhere in the city that's being targeted."

"Like witches and shit?"

"Far worse than witches, they're spreading like a disease, and not only among the homeless population. That's what I've heard, at any rate."

Marco snickers a little, but mostly because he's uncomfortable with where their conversation has gone. "Where do you get all this stuff, Billy?"

"I get around," he says with a wink. "But you know how urban legends are. It could very well all be nonsense, though something tells me this time it's anything but. And that is why you need to be careful. One can never be certain if such stories are just that, or if they possess a modicum of truth. Until, of course, one can."

"Well, I'm not worried about it. I'm not in any coven or whatever it's called and I'm not part of any disease. What would they want with me? I'll be fine."

"Let's talk about something else then." Billy sits back drunkenly and sips his drink. "So tell me, how is that pretty little girlfriend of yours?"

"Ginger? We broke up."

"I'm sorry to hear that."

"It's okay." Marco takes his eyes from the window because the swirling snow is making his head spin. "She decided to go out west for a while. She's got family there. We wanted different things."

"I see."

"She thinks I don't take life seriously enough," Marco says.

Billy watches him over the rim of his glass. "And what do *you* think? Do *you* think you take life seriously enough?"

"Not at all, but so what? I'm young and got my whole life ahead of me, right? Shit, the way I see it, Billy, this is exactly the time to have fun and *not* take things seriously. There'll be plenty of time for that later."

"I like the way you think."

They tap glasses again.

"She was very sexy, that...*Ginger*," Billy says.

Marco tosses back the rest of his drink. "Hot as fuck and really sweet too, a nice girl. I'm just not ready to settle down yet."

"And why should you be?" Billy powers down the remainder of his drink as well. "Did you know she came into the store once? We were running a big sale in the women's department. I fitted her for a dress. It needed alterations. She told me she had trouble finding things off the rack that fit her properly. No wonder, she's such a tiny little thing. Nice tits on the cunt, though."

Marco isn't sure he heard Billy correctly, and his mind is slow to catch up. He didn't expect Billy to say such a thing, but he realizes now just how drunk they both are. *Fuck it*, he thinks. *No harm no foul.*

"They had some nice weight to them," Billy says. "Ginger's tits, I mean."

He wonders if the old man might be toying with him now. Marco's not sure if he should laugh or just listen, so he chooses the latter and waits to see what Billy might say next.

"Trust me, tailors get away with murder." Billy leans closer, his black eyes bleary and his speech beginning to slur. "I've felt up more people in the course of doing my job than I can count. You'd be surprised how easy it is. Ginger didn't even flinch when I handled and lifted those tits, or when I ran my hand over that tight little ass of hers. I just keep talking like all is right with the world and this is how it's done and most people go along with it. Isn't that something?"

Marco tests the waters with a cautious smile. "Are you messing with me?"

"Not at all," he says. "I'm *very* familiar with her body, believe me."

"That's wild," Marco says, though quietly.

"I hope you're not upset with me." Billy theatrically bats his eyes like some silent movie star. "I'm quite drunk, and when I get this way I often say things I probably shouldn't."

"Don't worry about it, just two guys talking."

"You mean two *friends* talking."

"Sure, Billy, two friends."

"I didn't offend you then?"

"Nah, we're not even together anymore." Marco knows that shouldn't matter, but he's not sure how else to move on to another topic. "So anyway—"

"Good," Billy says with a mischievous grin. "You already fucked the little slut every way possible, so why give a damn now, right?"

"Yeah," he says. "Anyway, I hope she finds what she's looking for."

Billy crosses his legs and leans forward. "And what about you, Marco?"

"Me?"

"What are *you* looking for?"

Marco looks at his empty glass while he thinks about it.

"You're not entirely sure, are you?"

It's not really a question, and Marco realizes this, but he answers anyway. "No, I guess not. I'm still finding my way, you could say."

Billy's devilishly black eyes sparkle in the limited light of the apartment. "Aren't we all, my friend," he says, slowly licking his lips.

"I should probably get going soon." Marco's vision blurs a bit, and the room tilts then corrects itself. He rubs his eyes and adjusts his position on the loveseat. "Jesus, I'm really totaled."

"As am I, so the damage is already done." Billy gives his knee a quick pat, then takes the empty glass from him and crosses back into the kitchen. "Which, correct me if I'm wrong, means there's really no good reason not to have one more nice stiff drink for the road."

Marco doesn't feel like moving. In fact, if he could just sink deeper into the cushions of the loveseat, he might even drift off to sleep. But he knows he can't do that or he'll be here all night, so he forces himself to his feet.

He almost loses his balance but manages to catch himself on the arm of the loveseat enough to stay upright. "I don't know, I think it may be Uber time."

"I hope you can get one in this storm," Billy says, suddenly at his side again with a fresh drink. He holds it out for Marco. "Go ahead, take it."

Marco does. "Okay, one more for the road then I got to go."

As he moves to the side of the loveseat, Billy motions to the projector. "Would you still like to see some of my movies?"

"Sure," Marco says, staggering to his left and looking at the screen. "Isn't there supposed to be film in there or something?"

"It's not a film projector," Billy explains. "It projects VHS tapes up onto the screen there."

"VHS for like VCRs and shit like that? Jesus, I didn't think they even made those anymore. I'm not sure I've ever seen one in real life."

Billy smiles coyly. "Real life," he says. "It's an endlessly interesting concept, but one that should never, under any circumstances, be confused with *projections*. Don't you agree?"

"To be honest," Marco slurs, "I'm so shitfaced right now, dude, I don't know what the fuck you're talking about."

"No. Not yet."

Marco realizes then that he has a fresh drink but Billy didn't make another for himself too. "Look, Billy," he says, his head spinning. "I need to finish this drink and call for a ride. I like you, man, you're a good guy. Little out there sometimes, but it's cool. I just don't want you to think I'm staying or—well—that I want something more. You get what I mean?"

"You're saying you don't want to have sex with me."

"Yeah," Marco says, holding his glass up a moment before taking a long sip. "No offense."

"None taken." Billy moves over to the camcorder on the filing cabinets and hits a button on it. The side pops open with a buzz and a loud clunking sound. He reaches inside and pulls free a VHS cassette, which he then walks over and slides into the projector.

"I mean, if I was gay or bi or whatever you are, it'd be cool, but I'm not."

Billy glides over to the apartment door then stops and looks back at Marco. He no longer seems to be having trouble walking. In fact, he no longer looks drunk at all. "I hate to ruin such a kind explanation, Marco, but while like anyone else I have many desires, and yes, they're quite *varied*, let's say, as you'll see in my movies, I'm merely an observer. I've never been one for rules. I find them wholly unnecessary and horribly restrictive. In fact, I encourage you to ignore them too. But, that said, all I ever do is watch and keep a record. And I've been doing that with you for a very long time now. How could I not?"

A sharp pain pierces Marco's stomach but passes quickly. "I don't get it. You've been watching me?"

"Oh yes, for quite some time now."

"Watching me how? What do you mean?"

"What do you think I mean?"

"You're like a, what do they call it, a *voyeur*?"

"Something along those lines, yes." Billy opens the door. "But right now I'm afraid you'll have to excuse me. I need to use the restroom. Why don't you relax, make yourself comfortable? I'll be back in a jiff!"

Billy leaves, quietly closing the door behind him before Marco can question him further.

Stumbling over to the loveseat, Marco reaches for his jacket, which he has left draped over the arm. He doesn't remember taking it off but he must have at some point. As he slides his hand into the side pocket in search of his phone, a series of flashes on the screen on the wall catch his attention.

The screen goes dark then light then dark again in a continuing pattern, creating a strobe effect that encompasses the entire apartment. It makes Marco even dizzier and a little sick to his stomach, so he turns away. He goes for his phone again when his eyes land on the file cabinets against the far wall.

He wonders how long Billy might be.

After a quick look at the door, he staggers over to the cabinets and tries the drawer on the first of the two. Unlocked, it glides right open to reveal a dozen or more VHS tapes stacked inside. None are labeled or have any markings that might identify what they are, so Marco pushes the drawer closed and tries the second cabinet.

It is unlocked as well, but inside he finds a series of hanging manila folders, each labeled with a black marker. Marco rubs his eyes but can't get them to focus completely, so he leans in for a closer look.

He flips through the files, past various names that seem oddly familiar but he cannot place. Just as he's about to give up he sees what he feared most. No last name, just his first, written in bold black letters along the tab of one folder.

MARCO

After another quick glance at the door, he puts his drink down on the cabinet then carefully pulls the file free. Inside are a stack of black-and-white photographs that appear to be stills from a video. Most have been taken from a bit of a distance, some at the mall, some near his apartment, and others on the streets of the city. As he flips through to the final photograph, his hand begins to shake. It was taken from inside his apartment, from a corner of his bedroom.

"What the fuck," Marco whispers.

In the photograph he is sitting nude on the edge of his bed, smoking a cigarette and looking down at the floor with bleary eyes. Ginger stands in the doorway. Topless, she appears to be fresh out of the shower, one towel wrapped around her waist and another on her head. She is staring right at the camera, as if she can see Billy standing there taking it, and glares in a way Marco has never before seen her do. A lit cigarette hangs from her mouth.

But Ginger doesn't smoke, he thinks, *and how could he have been in my room and taken this without me knowing?*

Trembling, Marco returns the photographs to the file and tosses it on top of the cabinet. Scooping up his drink, he gulps it down then grabs the phone from his jacket and quickly finds the Uber app.

Fear, along with the strobing on the screen, even out of the corner of his eye, makes him feel as if he might pass out.

I got to get the fuck out of here.

He hits the wrong keys a few times but finally drunkenly manages to get his correct address into the app before realizing he doesn't know where he is. He has no idea what Billy's address is, how can he enter it in and tell a driver where to pick him up?

Fuck it, he thinks. *I'll take my chances in the snow and cold and hope there's still a taxi or two out there.*

Marco pulls on his jacket and is stumbling toward the door when it opens and Billy steps back inside.

"Leaving so soon?"

"Yeah, I'm out, I—I got to go."

Billy's eyes dart about, land on the file cabinets. He smiles, only now it seems far more threatening. "I see you've been snooping."

"You're one to talk. How the fuck did you get in my apartment?"

"I told you I've been watching," he says evenly. "I don't really have any choice, it's what I do. But there's no reason for you to snoop. You may look through any of the files or watch any of the tapes you'd like. They all originate from one mind anyway. Yours."

"What?" Marco shakes his head. "What the fuck are you talking about? And how the hell did you get in my place?"

More amused than threatened, Billy says, "You let me in."

"No I didn't, you've never been to my apartment, I—"

"Don't you remember?"

"Fuck this," Marco says, waving a hand at him dismissively. "I'm leaving, I'm out—I just want to get out of here, man."

"But the fun is just beginning."

Marco tries to steady himself, but he's so drunk and so upset he just stumbles about awkwardly. "Look, Billy, I don't know what the fuck's going on here, but I'm out. *Out*, you got me? I don't want to hurt you, man, so get out of my way."

"Don't be ridiculous, the movie's almost ready to begin." Billy motions to the screen. "And besides, there's someone here to see you."

Billy steps away from the doorway, then flips a wall switch and the lights go off, leaving only that which emanates from the projector and the screen.

Heels clacking floor, another figure walks into the apartment, moving through the shadows in the hallway and into the strobing light.

As Billy closes the door, Marco sees a middle-aged woman standing before him. With gray hair pulled up into a bun atop her head, black eyeglasses, an ankle-length skirt, old-fashioned blouse with a high neck and lacy sleeves, and sensible lace-up shoes, she looks like someone from an earlier era.

Like something out of an old black-and-white horror movie, Marco thinks.

"What the fuck is going on?" he asks. "Did you put something in my drinks? Am I tripping balls here or what?"

Billy laughs hysterically, but the woman simply stares at him, her pale face expressionless.

For the first time she looks familiar to Marco, even bathed in the constant strobe light. "Who are you?" he asks.

"Don't you know me?"

Marco slowly shakes his head. "No, ma'am."

"As I told you once before," the woman says in a stern voice. "You may call me *Mrs. Milken.*"

"Sit down, boy," Billy says with a lascivious grin. "It's show time!"

CHAPTER 25

THE STROBE LIGHT CEASES, AND THE apartment is plunged into darkness.

Marco tries to find his way, looking to the window to get his bearings. He can see the snow falling peacefully through the night just beyond the thin pane of glass. If he can somehow escape into it, he knows the darkness will hide him from these people and—

The film comes to life on the large screen, filling the room with enough light for Marco to see Billy and the woman standing by the door. Their eyes are glued to the movie, as if they've become hypnotized by the images.

Marco turns, looks over his shoulder at the screen. Everything tilts and sways, he's so drunk. *Why—why did I let myself get so drunk?*

Images flash in montages before him, changing so fast one to the next that he cannot make out what he's looking at.

And then the picture turns to snow and static.

The movie flickers back to life, and he sees what appears to be his apartment, shot from the perspective of his bedroom. The bed is mussed and clothes are strewn about the floor. In the doorway is the silhouette of a woman.

After a moment, she steps into full view. Completely nude, she looks right at the camera and gives an angry leer.

"Ginger," Marco hears himself utter.

She pulls at her hair. It comes away in her hand, falls right off her head to reveal a shock of short black hair beneath. The woman drops the blonde wig to the floor and roughly runs her hands through her pixie cut, purposely mussing it. Her eyes are covered with heavy black eye makeup, and ruby red lipstick adorns her lips. Still staring at the camera, she raises her other hand.

She's holding a large knife.

Marco staggers about, wanting to look away. But he can't.

The woman…there's something wrong with her…

Marco finally manages to turn away and stumble toward the door. "Let me out!" he screams. "Let me out! You can't do this to me! Not to *me*!"

"Poor boy," Billy says. "You're so perfect, aren't you? Handsome and smart and strong, funny and kind, with loving parents and a nice home, a beautiful sexy girlfriend everyone else wants, a whole life ahead of you that will be filled with the advantages you always wanted but never had. He's everything you wish you could be if you could start again, isn't he? His life is laid out exactly as you'd do it if you could. Because you can, and did."

Mrs. Milken steps closer to him. "But that's over with now."

"What do you mean?" he asks, emotion choking him as a horrible stabbing pain rifles through his skull. "What do you mean *he's* everything I wish I could be? I *am* him, he is me!"

"Don't you understand you've broken enough rules?" Mrs. Milken asks. "Do you really think you can hide and pretend there will be no consequences for such actions?"

The film switches to a shot of a foggy rural road. It is empty and eerie, shot in black-and-white, and looks like a scene from a horror film. Slowly, through the fog, a small bus appears. The word RESIDENTS is painted on the side. As the bus moves past, Marco sees that the driver is obscured but there is a single passenger inside. A woman, she stares out one of the windows, her face pale, awash in sorrow.

Something about this woman causes Marco's legs to buckle, and he drops to his knees. The pain in his head grows stronger, and he presses his hands flat against his temples, fearful his skull may break apart otherwise.

"What is this?" he screams. "What's happening to me?"

Billy and Mrs. Milken stand behind him, eyes transfixed on the screen.

The same woman from the bus appears again. Her face fills the entire screen. Smoke curls across the frame, signaling the person filming is smoking. As the camera pulls back, the woman comes into full view. She is nude, and this makes Marco want to vomit, though he doesn't quite understand why, because although the woman appears deeply damaged, she is also quite beautiful.

And I know her. I don't know how, but I know her.

"Just as she knows you," Billy whispers.

A man steps into frame and kneels before the woman, forcing her legs apart before he begins to fuck her.

"Please," Marco says, gagging. "Make it stop."

The film goes to snow again but quickly reverts. This time the same woman is standing in a small apartment, looking directly at the camera. She has auburn hair, milky white skin, and a petite build. Marco's eyes fill with tears because he thinks she is the most beautiful woman he has ever seen.

"What are you going to do to me?" the woman asks, looking at someone off camera.

"Cleanse you, baby," a male voice answers. "I'm going to make you whole. It's time."

The woman hugs herself. She can't seem to stop shaking.

"It's time to be reborn," the man says.

Marco screams like never before. The pain stabbing through his head becomes unbearable.

And he begins to understand...

Flashes—blood and flesh—raw meat running with bloody juices—shadowy figures tearing at it with their talons and fangs—groans and growls and moans of ecstasy—screams, bloodcurdling screeches—the night—fog—the city streets empty and covered in snow—fire—flames exploding and rising, filling the darkness—chanted prayers hideous and profane—

What appears to be a liquor store appears onscreen. Marco's mind is a tempest of confusion and horror as he tries to stand, fails, and through the blur of his tears, looks to the scene playing out before him.

Shot from the shadows at the rear of the store, a man pushes through the door and moves over toward the counter. Marco *knows* this man, he—

"Where am I?" he sobs, falling forward to the floor. "Am I in Hell?"

Marco clenches shut his eyes and refuses to sit up and look anymore. He won't watch and they can't make him. But he can still hear the movie playing.

"You sleep now."

He feels a powerful hand grab his hair and yank. His head snaps up but he keeps his eyes closed.

"It's okay to sleep."

"Look at it," Billy growls in his ear. "Fucking *look at it!*"

Shaking uncontrollably, Marco opens his eyes…and sees.

Stringer plunges the knife into Owen's belly until his thumb strikes wet flesh. He's buried the blade clear up to the handle. With both hands gripping the knife, Stringer stands, dragging the blade with him and tearing Owen's abdomen straight up to the sternum.

With everything he has, Marco shakes free of Billy's grip and rises to his feet. He turns, swinging, but Billy has already retreated and stands over by the file cabinets.

"I want to go home," Marco cries out, spittle drooling from his mouth.

Mrs. Milken moves closer. "You are home." The woman's dead eyes hold his stare. "Do you see now what breaking the rules has gotten you?"

"Get out of my way or I'll kill you."

From the corner of his eye, Marco sees Billy slowly reach for the camcorder, put it on his shoulder, and begin to record.

"We're one," she says. "You can't kill me without killing yourself. Don't you know that by now? You, and Billy and I…we are one."

Marco lunges for her, grabbing her by the throat with such force they both fall back to the floor. He lands on top of her, and although she squirms about beneath him and tries to dislodge his grip, he is far too powerful for her.

Moving closer, Billy continues to record, as Marco squeezes harder, his face twisted in murderous rage as Mrs. Milken's eyes bulge and spittle begins to froth and bubble from her mouth.

"That's it," Billy tells him. "Kill the cunt! Kill her!"

A moment later, he has.

Marco falls off of her and staggers toward the door. With his heart smashing his chest and his head spinning, he looks back at Billy. A cigarette dangles from his lips, the smoking rising through the air and catching the light from the projector. He's still recording.

"We're free of her now."

Breathing heavily, Marco wipes the drool from his mouth with the back of his hand. "We…"

Slowly, Billy lowers the camcorder. "You and I, of course," he says, pointing to his temple. "Just like Milken, I'm all up here. The three pieces of your mind, do you understand now? I am the impulsive one that needs to be kept under control because I have none myself. That dead board-up-her-ass bitch was the staunchly moral and rational one who tries to keep us all in line. And you…you are the personality from which we all come, the one who tries to find balance between us all, because that's what sane minds do. Even the insane try to accomplish it…with varied results, of course…but we're all pieces of one mind. One sick little head. Yours."

The world flickers around Marco like the movie on the screen.

"Remember what I told you?" Billy asks. "Real life is an endlessly interesting concept, but one that should never, under any circumstances, be confused with *projections.*"

Trembling, Marco nods.

"And you, beautiful perfect Marco, are nothing but."

As the pain returns, Marco feels like his skin is coming loose, as if it's being torn from his bones like rotted meat.

"We're all in here," Billy says again, tapping his temple with his index finger. "And you, *Joseph*, well, I'm afraid you're out there…with *them.*"

CHAPTER 26

THROUGH THE SCREAMS AND AGONY OF transformation, through the huge columns of fire exploding before him—smoke, great twisting columns of it billowing about and rising toward a blistering, unforgiving sky—the fire vanishes like a flashpoint, leaving behind a world of embers. And carried on winds hot and dry comes an awful smell he recognizes as the sweet and sickening stench of burning human flesh.

Shaking violently, his body quakes with impossible speed, as if throttled by unseen hands, shifting, changing, returning to origins he has tried so hard to forget and alter.

Billy watches through his camcorder lens, remembering it all for them both, and once the change is complete, he smiles and walks away, back to the shadows where he belongs, where he lives. Where he watches and waits.

Forever...

And then Joseph finds himself running along a narrow dirt passage, a tunnel burrowed long ago and deep into the sand to form a maze of sorts. The light from above shows him the way, and as he continues running, he stumbles, hitting the walls of the tunnels with his shoulders.

It is then that he sees her.

On her knees and clad in a long white gown stained with the grave, she looks back over her shoulder at him, blood smeared across her mouth and chin. "Don't look at me," she whispers, opening her mouth in a silent growl to reveal hideous fangs where her canines should be.

Joseph closes his eyes.

When he returns from the darkness, he finds himself on a lonely street in the city late at night. In the shadows, as heavy fog rolls along the dark street, she's there too, kneeling next to a fresh kill, the body bloody and torn to pieces. Her auburn hair drips blood, and wet crimson swaths cover her mouth, cheeks, and neck.

"Mother," he says from behind a veil of slowly creeping fog.

She glances at him, but continues to consider the kill before her. "Why did you come back here?" she asks.

Her voice is different than he remembers, different from his dreams.

"I've looked for you for years."

"I never wanted this for you. I sacrificed myself so you wouldn't have to endure an existence like mine."

"It was too late. I fought it for most of my life, but I'm the same as you."

"No," she says, bowing her head.

Horrible visions of his decaying father blink across his mind's eye. An old man lurching naked through the hallways of an old and forgotten apartment building, trapped in a gateway in a city of night, a city of destruction, a city of monsters.

And those who seek to destroy them.

"My father," Joseph says. "I still see him in my mind sometimes."

"Destroyed," she tells him. "Captured and burned years ago. The nest, it's mine now, but there aren't many of us left."

He remembers the fire…the agony…

"Witches aren't the only ones they burn," Carla says. "They've been killing our kind with fire for centuries."

"They're going to kill *me*, Mother."

"One day they'll kill us all." She looks up at the night sky, as if she's seen something for her eyes only. "Maybe that won't be such a bad thing. We don't belong in this world. We never did. We're just trapped like everyone else."

He wants nothing more than to put his arms around her, to feel the love and acceptance he once knew and has been searching for since childhood. "Can you save me?" he asks.

Dead eyes filled with sorrow, she slowly shakes her head. "Not anymore."

"I love you," Joseph tells her.

"And I love you, son."

He reaches for her, but as he does so, the night burns away, returning him to the desert and the tunnels that run through it.

Before he can touch her, she begins to slowly disintegrate and vanish in layers, like a sand sculpture assaulted by a dry and dangerous desert wind.

Joseph feels the hot winds blow, and knows now what they mean for him.

When his mother is gone, he finds himself kneeling where she once existed, clutching an old, dirty, tattered gown stained with blood. It smells of death, of evil, of ancient graves filled with the bones of things long dead.

He presses the garment to his chest and, rocking, begins to weep.

CHAPTER 27

THE FLAMES BURN THROUGH. The screams quiet. The pain drifts away.

And there is only a highway. Long and vast and dark, it is empty but for a single car that flies right down the center of its two blacktop lanes.

Behind the wheel, a young woman, strung out and wanting nothing more than to leave this place, to find something else, something better, something new, drops the windows despite the cold and slams the gas with her foot.

As the car speeds into the night, she smiles as cold winds blow her auburn hair about and water her already blurry eyes. Stoned and heartbroken, she knows now the man she loves is not coming back.

And yet she smiles.

Not with joy, but defiance.

Instinct tells her to slow her speed, to take care, but she ignores all that. She wants to go even faster, so fast that time will lose all meaning and she can vanish into this cold dark night littered with angels and demons alike.

Because the angels are not concerned with her tonight...

It is the demons that gather on her behalf.

Up ahead, a figure kneels on the side of the road. As she gets closer, she sees it is a middle-aged man in the breakdown lane. He is filthy and his clothes are tattered. *He must be homeless,* she thinks, *a nomad walking this lonely highway in search of…what?*

As she races past, she turns and looks his way, catching a better glimpse of the man while he is still illuminated by her headlights.

Hunched over the body of another man, or what was once a man, he raises his head and their eyes meet.

Blood covers his mouth and neck.

It is the last thing she remembers before losing control of the car and crashing into a guardrail.

The night, the car, and the woman come to a horribly sudden, violent stop.

She does not know this, as she's unconscious and bleeding from a wound in her abdomen. But she will dream, and she will come to know the mysteries of the darkness that even now swirls around her like the living thing it is.

And she will *become.*

A gentle snow begins to fall.

Somewhere on the other side of this night, this darkness, a helpless mutilated creature struggles beneath a wet blanket soaked in gasoline.

A match is thrown and fire engulfs it.

Pain…release…and then its world goes dark as a cold winter night on a desolate highway.

A car has smashed against a nearby guardrail with such force that it's become partially propped up on the twisted metal, the rear tires still spinning.

It watches a moment but doesn't understand. Not yet.

Soon it will reach the city. That is all that matters.

As a cloud slowly passes over the moon, it gazes up at the night sky with a longing only its kind can know, fangs glistening in the natural light.

Then it turns back to that which lies before it, and continues to feed.

A NOTE FROM THE AUTHORS

A small portion of Part One of this work features characters and situations (although vastly rewritten) that were originally published years ago in short story form in a piece entitled *Malevolent Night*, written by Greg F. Gifune.

ABOUT THE AUTHORS

GREG F. GIFUNE is a best-selling, internationally-published author of several acclaimed novels, novellas and two short story collections. Working predominantly in the horror and crime genres, Greg has been called, "The best writer of horror and thrillers at work today" by *New York Times* bestselling author Christopher Rice, "One of the best writers of his generation" by horror grandmaster Brian Keene, and "Among the finest dark suspense writers of our time" by legendary bestselling author Ed Gorman. Greg's work has been published all over the world, translated into several languages, received starred reviews from *Publishers Weekly*, *Library Journal* and others, and is consistently praised by readers and critics alike. His novel THE BLEEDING SEASON, originally published in 2003, has been hailed as a classic in the horror genre and is considered to be one of the best horror/thriller novels ever written. Two of his stories (HOAX and FIRST IMPRESSIONS) have been adapted into short films, and his novel LONG AFTER DARK is set to begin production as a feature film in 2021. Greg and his wife Carol reside in Massachusetts with their dogs, Dozer and Dudley. Greg can be reached online at gfgauthor@verizon.net or on Facebook, Twitter and Instagram.

* * * *

SANDY DeLUCA is an American author and visual artist, born in Providence, Rhode Island. As an author, she is known for dark and surreal prose; often visceral and shocking. She is best known for her work in the horror genre. She has produced critically acclaimed novels; DESCENT, MESSAGES FROM THE DEAD, and MANHATTAN GRIMOIRE.

She was a finalist for the Bram Stoker Award ® for poetry in 2001, with BURIAL PLOT IN SAGITTARIUS, accompanied by her cover art and interior illustrations. A copy is maintained in the Harris Collection of American Poetry and Plays (Brown University) Poetry, 1976-2000. She was also nominated once more in 2014, with Marge Simon, for DANGEROUS DREAMS.

She lives in New England with three feisty tortoiseshell cats. She is an avid book collector, spending her free time reading, researching family genealogy and studying the metaphysical.

www.ingramcontent.com/pod-product-compliance
Lightning Source LLC
Chambersburg PA
CBHW020339260626
47156CB00004B/1610

* 9 7 8 1 9 5 0 3 0 5 6 7 4 *